THE LIGHTS OF TIME

Enjoy j[ou]rney through
journey &
space-time!
Paul ⭒
— ⭒ —

PAUL IAN CROSS

Text © Paul Ian Cross 2018
First published in Great Britain in 2018

Farrow Children's Books
London
United Kingdom

Paul Ian Cross has asserted his right under the Copyright, Designs
and Patents Act 1988 to be identified as the author of this work.

Cover design and title lettering © Patrick Knowles Design
Cityscape © Shutterstock
Book designed by Maya Tatsukawa
Type set in Bitter

British Library Cataloguing in Publication data available.

Paperback ISBN: 978-1-912199-05-1
e-ISBNs: 978-1-912199-06-8 & 978-1-912199-07-5

To Mum and Nan, my guiding lights
on my own journey through space-time.

THE LAWS OF SCIENCE DO NOT DISTINGUISH
BETWEEN THE PAST AND THE FUTURE.

— Professor Stephen Hawking

2074-APR-12 23:37

NEW SHANGHAI CITY, ASIAN PROTECTORATE

Engella was tired; too tired to care where she'd sleep. Desperate for rest, she wandered through an alley until she found an alcove large enough to crawl inside. As she huddled against the damp brick wall, she covered herself in a plastic tarpaulin to protect herself from the rain.

Thunder rumbled. The torrent continued. Puddles and pools merged into rivers which criss-crossed the street, and Engella's clothes were soaked through. She pushed a few wet strands of her silver-dyed hair behind her ears and adjusted her hood, trying to limit the water dripping in. She sighed and accepted it was a pointless task. Her makeshift blanket hadn't helped.

A police drone zoomed high above. As it hovered and hummed, it scanned for movement in the streets below. It was probably chasing a thief it had identified, tracking them with its facial recognition software. Sirens whined and blue flashing lights danced across the metal scaffolding for a moment.

A long-haired black and white cat stepped out from behind a large metal container, staring at Engella with piercing eyes that reflected light from the streetlamps. He rubbed along the edge of the container before greeting Engella with a soft purr. Engella reached out and clicked her fingers to summon him. He padded over and allowed her to stroke his head, his purr more pronounced, now a soothing hum. The sound was calming and Engella rested her eyes.

The police drone returned, this time zipping right above their heads, and the cat – startled by the hum of the propellers – darted off into the night.

This was Engella's fourth night living on the streets of New Shanghai City and she hadn't felt this safe for months. She shuffled forwards to get a better view of the towering skyscrapers all around. Vast screens illuminated the cityscape, the buildings completely covered with screens of light. High-definition images flashed, alternating between human faces, commercial products and scenes of serene beauty. Her eyes were drawn higher to the levels of the city's upper dome, a place she dared not travel to. The security of the upper levels used biometric data to access transport, shops and even the street-food stalls, whereas the security on the streets of the lower districts was far less stringent. People from all walks of life could keep themselves to themselves in the low-levs.

The rain slowed, giving Engella some respite. Breathing a sigh of relief, she found a more comfortable position and began to drift off to sleep at last.

A few seconds passed before she realised what was happening. The dizziness took hold more slowly than usual, but the feeling of suffocation quickly engulfed her. Her pulse quickened. She froze, too frightened to move. The streetlamp above her flickered and the bulb cracked, sending tiny shards of glass cascading to the street.

Engella found herself in darkness. A tiny freckle of light appeared. And then another. And then the alleyway was flooded with noise and light. Flashes of orange rushed outward in waves as the space around her began to warp. She grabbed her ears in pain as a piercing hum pounded her eardrums and a sonic boom knocked her against the brick wall.

Shielding her eyes from the emerging light, she watched in horror as a dark figure materialised only metres away.

They've found me, she thought. *They're here.*

Engella rolled sideways, scraping her hands across the gravel as an energy blast hit the alcove where she'd been lying. She pushed herself off the ground and found herself sprinting, not waiting to see her assailant emerge from the veil of black smoke. She touched her belt, moving her fingers along the leather until they touched the cold metal of her blaster. She opened the clip and managed to draw the weapon, directing three bolts behind her.

She ran ahead, but a shock-grenade landed in her path. She yelped as the device exploded, showering her with brick and dust. After pulling back her sleeve, she waved her hand over her silver wristband to turn the transporter on. With no time to enter any coordinates, Engella had no way of knowing where – or when – she'd end up. She had no choice. She had to get away.

Closing her eyes, Engella hoped for the best. And prepared for the worst.

'Shift!' she yelled.

The device bleeped, and space-time warped around her.

Another shock-grenade exploded, but this time the sonic boom knocked the wind from her lungs. Her senses were overwhelmed. All that remained was the ringing in her ears and a spike of pain in her forehead.

The pain became too much.

Her vision blurred, and she lost consciousness.

α β ϕ

1998-JAN-22 16:07
RUBHA SHLÈITE, SKYE, SCOTLAND

Engella opened her eyes, awoken by the distant crash of waves. She found herself on her side, her face pressed against the cold ground. She could feel damp clumps of sand between her fingers and a cool spray in the air. It wasn't long before she realised she'd arrived on a beach, and that it was intensely cold.

As she lifted her head, she scanned the surrounding area. Pieces of brick and dust lay in the sand. They must have been caught in the portal as she shifted away. The Hunters had never made it so close before. Their attacks were becoming more targeted, finding her location in space-time with improved accuracy. At least it had taken them several weeks to find her this time. Yet, it was a concern she couldn't brush away lightly.

Engella sighed. 'Still wet,' she said.

Rolling onto her back, she gazed at the sky. The cumulus clouds looked like candyfloss. A freezing wave splashed over her, forcing her to focus on the task ahead.

'Time to move,' she muttered.

The beach was relatively silent except for the squawks of seagulls hovering on the upwind. It was late afternoon; the sun was low and the sky was turning pink.

Engella dawdled along the sand, her cape catching the wind. She placed her hand on her belt, and then reached inside her rucksack, eager to check she hadn't lost any of her gadgets or supplies.

The chilly air began to bite. Feeling uncomfortable in the cold, she wrapped her long coat tightly around her body. In addition to her braces and black T-shirt, she wore a grey-tinted utility belt fitted with various objects, cargo pants and black boots with silver laces. Engella was particularly proud of her belt and lace combination. She'd chosen the colours to match her current choice of hair colour. Silvers, greys and a dash of purple too. Super stylish. After years on the run, many of them on the streets, Engella still knew how to accessorise.

The wind picked up, and Engella shivered, so she lifted the hood of her cape covering her hair. The waves tumbled over the shore with a splash. White foam washed away to reveal glistening sand which reflected light from the sunset. She remembered how she'd always loved the beach as a child; going on day trips with her parents, building sandcastles, and eating ice cream. It was always a treat to get away from London's metropolis.

Engella remembered her mother's face.

'At least the weather's better here,' she said. She paused as her favourite holomovie came to mind, *The Wizard of Oz*. She smirked as she thought of a quote which was appropriate for the situation.

'We're not in Kansas anymore, that's for sure.'

Engella had always pretended to be the little girl with the pet dog while her father took on the role of the Tin Man. She reached for her wristband, anxious to check it was still there, and was relieved to feel the cold metal between her fingers. A red warning light flashed, so she clicked the reset button. Engella had never shifted through space-time without coordinates before, so she didn't know what it meant.

Along the beach, a figure came into view. Engel-

ⅅ α β

la's neck prickled. She usually tried to avoid people, it was easier that way, even though she often pined for human contact. The loneliness had continued for too long. Using a device which she removed from her utility belt, Engella scanned the area to identify the approximate space-time coordinates. She didn't have time to find the exact date, but the scan quickly determined it to be sometime in the late twentieth century.

As she activated her holoprojector, her real clothes were quickly concealed by a hologram: a grey hooded jumper, black jeans and black Converse trainers, which suited the timeframe perfectly. Her plaited hair was now neatly placed inside a holographic pink bobble hat. She looked at her reflection briefly, using the metal of her wristband as a mirror.

'Retro!' she said.

As they approached each other, Engella could now make out the other person: an older woman, walking a chocolate Labrador who was splashing through the surf. They eventually met halfway along the beach.

'Good evening, dear,' the woman said, as she surveyed Engella through her black spectacles. She was probably in her fifties, her curly brown hair greying at the roots. Her skin was pale white, yet she looked slightly red-faced and flustered, wrapped up in her winter coat and scarf. The Labrador bounded towards Engella, panting and tail-wagging, and sniffed her holographic trainers.

'Sorry about Rupert! He does get overexcited now and then!' the woman said.

Engella patted Rupert on the head. 'It's okay. He's very sweet.'

'We don't often get visitors around here, you see.'

Engella nodded. 'Where exactly is *here* by the way? I'm a little lost.'

'Rubha Shlèite, dear. My favourite place on the Isle of Skye.'

'The sky?' said Engella, a little unsure of what she'd heard. 'Erm, yes, of course. I remember now.' Engella pretended to know what the woman was talking about, but she had no idea.

'Did you travel here via the road or by ferry?' asked the woman, who then proceeded to rearrange her scarf so it was almost touching her bottom lip.

Engella looked away, not sure how to answer. She had hoped she wouldn't need to explain her sudden appearance. Although she was used to it by now. It wasn't the first time and it wouldn't be the last either.

Travelling through space-time was fraught with challenges. Engella would often arrive in unusual places. For example, there was one time when she turned up in the middle of a family's dining room during dinner. On another occasion, she'd shifted above a busy lake, full of rowing boats and people who happened to be rowing them. Now that one had certainly caused a splash. Possibly the worst time of all was when Engella shifted inside one of the cars of a moving ghost train, in an amusement park in Florida. The poor children who were seated in the front of the carriage received such a terrible fright that Engella wondered if they'd ever ride a ghost train again. Hence, it was much easier to avoid other people altogether. But sometimes it just wasn't possible.

Fortunately for Engella, this place didn't seem to have too many people around to notice a girl materialising out of thin air. Engella looked out along the beach. The place name the woman had mentioned, 'sky', sounded familiar, so Engella thought back to her geography lessons. She remembered now. Could this place be the Isle of Skye, in Scotland? The woman's accent certainly sounded Scottish, so that made sense.

Shanghai to Scotland was only a short trip, especially when shifting through a wormhole. Folding space-time made travelling between two points, however far apart, simple and incredibly fast.

Engella considered the other places she could have ended up, perhaps even further north than here, like the Arctic. Now that *would* have been cold.

'The ferries haven't been running for two days, dear. The weather has been terrible. A few major storms have hit the island lately. Did you have trouble getting over the bridge? They close it when the wind picks up too much.'

Engella reached out to Rupert again, patting his back until he rolled onto his side, and managed to avoid the question.

'Oh, he likes you! He's not usually like this with strangers,' the woman said with a warm smile. 'What's your name, dear?'

'Engella.'

'That's a beautiful name. I'm Annys.'

'Pleased to meet you, Annys,' Engella said, as she looked the woman directly in the eyes. She had a gentleness about her, and Engella felt at ease.

'You're not from around here, are you?' Annys said, as she placed her hand on Rupert's head.

'No, I'm just visiting. I'm originally from London.'

The wind began to stir, and a gust of wind almost knocked them off their feet. They laughed, as the strength of the wind rushed at them, forcing them to adjust their footing and stop themselves being blown away.

'Strong, isn't it?' Annys said with a grin. 'These gusts could knock over a lorry!'

Engella smiled, while still struggling to maintain her balance. She'd never experienced anything quite like it. The wind died down again and Engella shivered in her wet clothes, clothes she knew looked perfectly dry to Annys.

'You must be freezing,' Annys said. 'It's very late. Are you here with your parents?'

'No, I'm travelling alone.'

Annys's expression changed to one of concern. 'Please tell me to mind my own business, but what is a girl of your age doing alone on the beach at this time of day? You can't be older than sixteen.'

'I'm seventeen, actually.'

Engella tried to remember the last time she'd celebrated her birthday. She couldn't remember. In fact, she hardly knew what day it was at all, let alone when her birthday was. She'd often make notes in her journal to keep track of dates, but she hadn't been able to write an entry for a while. Shifting through space-time made it harder and harder to remember. She was beginning to lose track of time.

'Do you know what day it is?' Engella asked.

'Are you feeling okay? Have you had a bump on the head or something? Well, it's Thursday.'

'The date?

Annys now looked even more concerned. 'It's January, dear. Erm, let me think. It's the 22nd ... January 22nd 1998.'

Engella's eyes widened. She'd travelled back in time further than ever before. Seventy-six years. The further back in time she travelled, the further away she'd be from home. Engella didn't know how to react and Annys, sensing something wasn't right, put her arm around Engella's shoulders.

'My dear, why don't you come back to the cottage for a cup of tea? It's only a few minutes' walk away.'

Engella opened her mouth to speak, and almost rejected the offer outright. But she held back and considered it carefully. She looked into the woman's big blue eyes and felt strangely at ease with her, even though they'd only just met.

Engella had learnt at an early age to avoid strangers at all costs. With the Hunters always on her tail, she couldn't risk trusting the wrong person. There was always the chance that she'd come across an agent in disguise. And it wasn't only the Hunters that Engella needed to watch out for. There was also the complex network of spies who provided intelligence; who observed and listened from within the shadows, ready to alert the Hunters with any information they came across, so the Hunters could continue their chase.

Engella had, however, learned to trust her gut, which had served her well over the years. She decided it couldn't hurt to go with the woman, if only for an hour or so. At the very least, she would have the opportunity to dry her clothes and warm up properly. All she'd known since she was a child was a life on the run, as she drifted from place to place. Engella thought about her parents again and how she'd been separated from them all those years before. Still, this was not a time to be sad. It was about time that something good happened, she deserved it. Her mind drifted and before long, she realised that the woman had been waiting patiently for her reply.

'I suppose it'll be okay for a while. Yes. Thank you. I'd like that.'

Although, Engella couldn't let down her guard down, not for a second. One lesson she'd learned the hard way was that her situation could change at any moment. There was a near and present danger at all times. Engella was so used to this harsh reality that she hardly even noticed that she was always primed and alert; ready for any eventuality.

Annys led the way across the beach. Engella followed, her feet sinking deep into the sand as they walked to the point where the beach joined the hillside, a mix of sand, shrubs and grasses.

'This way,' Annys said as she pointed to a pathway which joined the beach. Annys held back, looking out for Rupert who was still on the beach. 'Come on, boy!' she yelled.

Rupert's ears pricked, yet he was more interested in a Fiddler crab he'd found. The crab was prepared to defend itself to the death, its claws raised like a knight lifting his shield for battle. Rupert soon became bored and allowed the poor crab to scurry away, able to fight another day. It hadn't been long before Rupert realised his owner and her new friend were out of sight. He barked and bounded back along the beach, running as fast as he could to reach them.

They'd been walking for fifteen minutes when the sun finally disappeared below the horizon. A full moon shone like a white beacon in the evening twilight. Engella marvelled at its beauty, untouched as it then was by colonists or mining corporations. Most of the lunar surface had been sold off to multi-planetary companies by the time Engella had been born, in the late twenty-first century. This view was different to the one familiar to Engella. All she could see when she looked at the moon from her bedroom window were the vast lunar cities, covered in a multitude of sparkling lights. The barren landscape of the moon in this time period had a strange beauty to it. She couldn't take her eyes off it.

Engella's gaze returned to the pathway which meandered through the trees.

Annys hurried on ahead while Rupert raced through the undergrowth, barking at the birds he'd flushed out of the bushes.

At the heart of a small wood, they arrived at a clearing. Engella emerged from behind an oak tree to see a small cottage covered in ivy. A wooden fence surrounded an immaculate garden, while rose bushes enclosed the neatly mowed lawn. The gate creaked and then slammed shut, startling Rupert.

'It's okay, darling!' Annys said, as she patted him on the head.

'You have a lovely garden,' Engella said.

'Home, sweet home,' said Annys, as she unlocked the door.

Engella followed Annys into the sitting room. The stove still had a few glowing cinders, which were trying to hold on. Annys picked up a pair of tongs and placed some more coals inside. She stuffed in some newspaper and tossed in a lit match. Flames licked around, and the newspaper quickly turned into a mini inferno. The coals began to glow and Engella relaxed as the room warmed.

'That's better,' Annys said, as she closed the door. 'You can't stop shivering, dear. Maybe you should put on something warmer? Hold on, I'll be right back.'

Annys left Engella to enjoy the warmth of the fire for several minutes, before returning with a pile of freshly ironed clothes.

'Why don't you change into these? And then, once you're ready, we can have a cup of tea together. The spare room is up the stairs, on the left. In fact, why don't you stay for dinner? You must be hungry.'

'I ... I don't know.'

'No questions asked, dear. You don't have to stay for long.'

'Okay, then. Yes. I'd like that.'

Engella stepped onto the wooden stairs which creaked under her weight. After finding the bathroom, she looked along the corridor to make sure she was still alone, before she switched off her holoprojector. She closed the bathroom door and changed out of her late twenty-first century outfit into the clothes which Annys had provided. She used her cloak to conceal her blaster, and placed them both in a cupboard among a pile of sheets.

Engella returned to the warmth of the sitting room and sat on a wooden rocking chair, covering her legs with a cotton blanket. She rested briefly, and closed her eyes.

Annys called out from inside the kitchen. 'Dinner's ready,' she said.

Engella joined Annys to find she'd cooked up a meal of smoked haddock, potatoes, and broccoli. They sat down together at a wooden table in the middle of the room. The smell of the food was tantalising and Engella couldn't wait to get started.

'Go ahead,' Annys said, as she passed Engella a fork. Engella couldn't resist and began to gobble it up quickly. It didn't take her long to finish.

'That was delicious!' Engella said, as she finished the last piece of fish.

Annys got up from the table, walked over to the oven, and opened the door. She pulled out a large tray, and placed it on the kitchen counter. She'd prepared a freshly baked apple pie, and she served them both a slice with a dollop of clotted cream.

Engella salivated as it was placed in front of her. She took a bite.

Delicious.

She hadn't tasted anything so good for as long as she could remember. This was real apple pie, made from real apples. Not the synthesised food tablets she had been used to in her time.

'It's getting late, dear. I know you don't want to talk about your situation and I'm not going to make you. But do you have somewhere to stay tonight?'

Engella looked down at the floor. 'No, I don't have anywhere to go,' she said.

'Okay, well. That's it then. You're staying here. The guest room is already prepared. Why don't you go and take a bath? You look like you need to relax.'

'Thank you. I really appreciate everything you're doing for me,' Engella said.

After a few hours of relaxing in front of the fire, Engella thanked her new friend, said goodnight, and went to her room. She lay on the comfortable bed among the soft sheets and couldn't believe that her luck had finally taken a turn for the better. In addition to spending some quiet time alone, she used the opportunity to write in her journal, noting down the space-time coordinates she had visited and the events which had occurred. She sketched portraits of Annys and Rupert, and also drew a map of the beach where she'd met them both. She had always enjoyed art, and sketching in particular, and she had an incredible talent for it. Not only did she enjoy creating the art, but the images and journal entries she had made helped her keep track of time. It was always so difficult, otherwise.

After she was done, she lay on the bed and closed her eyes. New Shanghai felt like a very long way away, then she remembered that it didn't even exist yet. She thought about old Shanghai, the place beneath the floating city she knew so well. She wondered what the old city was like, and imagined the people that lived there, before drifting off into a deep slumber.

She dreamt of the beach, sandcastles, and her parents.

🕊   🕊   🕊

The next morning Engella rested in bed, and watched the flowered curtains as they drifted in the breeze. Suddenly, there was a crash from downstairs, followed by a clatter which sounded like several pots tumbling across the kitchen floor.

'Sorry about that, dear!' Annys shouted, from downstairs.

Engella chuckled to herself as she got dressed. After putting on her dry clothes, she reactivated her holoprojector. She opened the door to find a strong smell of coffee which had drifted across the landing, and finally joined Annys in the kitchen.

'Good morning, dear. Did you sleep well?' said Annys, who was stirring something on the hob. 'Well, until I dropped a whole cupboard of pots that is,' she said with a wink.

'Morning, Annys. Yeah, I did, thank you. To be honest, I don't think I've slept that well in ages.' She thought back to her time on the streets of New Shanghai, where she'd been lucky to get an hour's sleep before being woken up by something, whether it be a person, animal or, more often than not, a refuse-bot sweeping rubbish from the streets.

Rupert strolled over and nuzzled Engella's leg before licking her hand. It tickled, and she pulled away laughing.

'I hope you're hungry,' said Annys. 'I've made bacon, eggs and potato cakes.'

'Yum. That sounds great.'

Annys smiled. 'Would you like coffee or tea?'

'I'd love a coffee, thank you.'

Annys poured her a cup and passed her a small jug of milk. They sat together and chatted about movies, theatre and the other types of entertainment they both enjoyed. Engella remembered not to mention holomovies, as they hadn't been invented yet.

They were both excited to discover that they had similar tastes. In fact, *The Wizard of Oz* was also one of Annys's favourite movies. Annys helped Engella to remember all of the characters' names. She thought back to the holomovie she had played with her father. It turned out the character she often played was the main role, a girl named Dorothy. Engella smiled as she remembered how her papa used to make funny voices when he acted out the various scenes. His impression of the Cowardly Lion was second to none.

'I used to watch it with my grandfather,' Annys said, as she sipped her coffee.

Rupert's ears pricked, and he jumped up from the mat where he'd been curled up. He became agitated, and began to pace across the kitchen floor. It wasn't long before he began to growl.

'Oh, shush, Rupert,' Annys said. 'Be quiet, boy!'

She got up from the table and walked over to the dog, who was now barking loudly. 'What's gotten into you?' she said, as she patted him on the head, but he turned his head and snapped at her fingers.

'Rupert!' Annys said, raising her hand in authority. He growled again, and then ran to the front door where he continued to bark.

'What the...?' said Annys, as she chased him across the kitchen.

She turned around briefly to see Engella grab her temples in pain. She looked like she was about to topple from her chair.

'Engella!' Annys shouted, as she rushed towards the girl, reaching her just in time to keep her steady.

'My head,' said Engella. 'I feel dizzy.' The terrible feeling of suffocation she'd known too well came first, before a wave of nausea overwhelmed her.

Engella turned to Annys, her face full of despair. 'You need to get out of here, Annys, you need to run!'

'Don't be frightened, dear, I can handle it, whatever it is,' said Annys.

A sound from outside caught their attention, and Rupert jumped up against the door, his claws scraping the wood.

'Annys, don't!' Engella yelled, reaching out.

But it was too late. Annys had already approached the door.

A piercing white flash lit the cottage, and a loud bang vibrated through the floor. The blast from the shock-grenade was so powerful, Annys had been knocked to the ground, while Rupert lay silently under a pile of brick and stone.

Shards of wood had been blown across the kitchen and the air was thick with dust, making it difficult for Engella to breathe. She coughed and spluttered as she inhaled the dirty air, and her heart raced as a surge of adrenaline rushed through her.

The smoke settled.

Engella's breathing slowed, as a dark figure entered through the open wound of the doorway.

'You're a difficult person to keep track of,' the Hunter said, narrowing her eyes. Like Engella, she also wore a dark cloak, her locks of curly red hair protruding from beneath the hood. She was tall and slender, while her cheeks were white and freckled. She lifted her blaster rifle, and waited patiently for its automatic crosshairs to zero in on its target.

Engella tried to reach for her wristband, but she didn't stand a chance. The Hunter was already beside her, grabbing her hands before she was able to activate the transporter, and bound her hands tightly using yellow cord.

She snatched the device from Engella's wrist, placed it on the table and, using the butt of her blaster, smashed it into several pieces.

The Hunter pushed up against Engella, her eyes bulging so much they looked like they were about to pop out. 'I'm going to enjoy this,' she said.

Engella had always known it was only a matter of time before the Hunters found her, and she had already prepared for this day. Yet she was angry with herself. Not for being caught, as that was inevitable. But because she shouldn't have visited the cottage. And more importantly, she shouldn't have put Annys in jeopardy. Filled with guilt, her eyes began to well up.

'You didn't think you'd get away from me, did you?' the woman said. 'I almost caught you in New Shanghai. I was so close, but you managed to slip away. You're making me look bad to the Company. Well, I finally did it. It took me a while, but I finally tracked down your trail to this place. I don't know how you could have let your guard down, Engella. You were always so careful. But I knew you'd mess up, eventually.'

Engella felt like crying, but she needed to remain

calm. 'Why are you doing this?' she asked.

'The Company needs rid of you. You should never have tried to run. We always find people who run. The sad thing for you, Engella, is that we don't care if you're dead or alive. What's it going to be then?'

Engella found it difficult to find the right words. 'I ... I ...' She paused, and looked down at the floor. She had never been so scared in her life. She turned to look at her wristband, damaged beyond repair.

I'm not getting away this time.

Engella closed her eyes and her mother's face came to mind. She remembered the beach again. Those days with her parents had been the happiest days of her life. The realisation of what was about to come crashed into her mind like a freight train. The pain of never seeing them again became too much. A few seconds passed, and Engella was able to clear her mind. She relaxed as a wave of tranquillity settled her nerves. Her breathing slowed and she prepared for the inevitable. Peace, at last. She was tired of running anyway.

A deafening blast rocked the cottage as the weapon fired.

And then, silence.

The feeling of being blasted at close range didn't hurt nearly as much as Engella thought it would.

Slowly, she opened one eye to find the Hunter lying motionless on the floor. She gasped as she saw Annys standing there, with Engella's blaster in her hands.

Annys composed herself, before running over to untie Engella's hands.

'I knew this would come in handy. I'm glad you're not very good at hiding things, dear. I should have organised the delivery of my own, really. Terribly careless, especially when I knew we were bound to have visitors,' Annys said.

Engella was speechless. She couldn't take her eyes off Annys.

Annys now looked quite different to the person who Engella had met the day before. She appeared shrewd and confident. It was as though a mask had been lifted. Once the initial shock had subsided, Engella was more intrigued than anything.

'This won't be the last of them, Engella. More of them will come,' Annys said. 'And it won't be long before this place is overrun with Hunters. We need to get away from here and we need to go soon.'

Annys opened the pantry door and reached inside, pulling out a rucksack. It appeared as though she had already packed the bag, as it was partially full. She began to open the kitchen drawers, and threw in a few additional supplies. Engella turned towards Rupert who was still and silent.

Annys noticed, and stopped what she was doing. She edged closer and reached out to her friend sombrely, stroking his back. 'I'm sorry, boy,' she said.

'I'm sorry about Rupert,' Engella said looking down.

'It's not your fault, dear.'

'I don't know what's going on here, but I'm grateful for what you did. But, I need to ask? Who are you? And why did you help me?' Engella asked.

'I've been waiting for you, Engella. We couldn't bring you out ourselves, but we managed to have your shiftband programmed with an override that would bring you here if you shifted without coordinates. It was the best we could do.'

'Shiftband? I don't understand.'

'You will, my dear. You're a very important person, Engella. I'll explain everything, I promise. But now, we need to go.'

Annys pulled back her sleeve to reveal her own metal wristband.

'How is this possible?' Engella asked, stunned.

'I'm sorry I couldn't tell you sooner. I needed to draw out any Hunters on your tail first. I'm your Watcher, Engella. You're no longer alone, I promise.'

Annys reached out, and took Engella by the hand. 'Hold on tight dear, this may be a bumpy ride. I haven't used it in a while,' she said.

For the first time in as long as she could remember, Engella felt truly protected. Safe. As she waved her hand over her wristband, Annys said, 'Shift.'

The space around them began to warp. A vibrant, aqua wormhole opened across the kitchen like a crack in an eggshell.

The portal engulfed them, and they were gone.

Lera Tox squinted, and shielded her eyes from the glare of the wormhole. The space around her warped as a whirlwind of photons faded away. Once the portal had finally closed, her eyes were able to focus on her surroundings. She could feel the softness of the sand as it crunched beneath her boots. It didn't take her long to realise she had shifted to a coastline; as she was stood a few hundred feet away from a beach.

A gust rushed over her half-shaven head, and her quiff-like mohawk of jet-black hair swayed in the breeze. She wore a charcoal fitted jumpsuit, while the only inks of colour on her entire body were a flash of silver around her neck, a pendant her mother had given her as a gift, and an opal bracelet, both pieces a nod to their Ethiopian heritage. The life she had lived in Lalibela, her childhood home, was now no more than a distant memory. In fact, she didn't recognise that person anymore.

She could taste sea salt in the air. The ocean crashed; the waves were choppy and the wind was gaining strength. She flipped open her V-Dis, and prepared to get to work.

'Initiate,' Lera said, as she activated the device. 'Scan for any undocumented wormhole activity.'

The V-Dis chimed, as it acknowledged her command. A three-dimensional projection of space-time appeared in line with Lera's field of vision. She lifted her opal bracelet to reveal the shiftband underneath, before noting the space-time coordinates and adjusting her holographic clothing to suit the place and time.

Her V-Dis was not only lightweight, but its visual display allowed her to view the distinct types of particle in the surrounding space. She was most interested in quarks: the most common particle formed as a by-product of wormhole activity.

Lera paced, unsure which way to go. Tala, Lera's commander, had decided to travel ahead against Lera's advice, but they'd lost the trail and it had taken them longer to find her coordinates than they had originally planned. However, Tala had managed to transfer her space-time coordinates to the Hunters' network before she had disappeared. But it had now been several hours since the time she was due to report in, and Lera was becoming increasingly concerned.

The whole situation made Lera tense. She kept one of her hands free at all times, making sure to rest her fingers on the tip of her utility belt; ready to pull out her blaster at the first sign of trouble. She held her V-Dis at arm's length, and pointed the device towards the crashing waves, watching as the space-time data flooded in. Holographic graphs and symbols crawled around the projection like a swarm of tiny insects.

The device whirred as it completed its analysis of the landscape. After completing the scan of one place, she'd hurry to the next. It wasn't long before she'd completed a full 360-degree turn. Eventually, she reached a point facing inland, when suddenly, the graphical projection spiked.

Lera's scowl turned into a grin. 'Result,' she said, over the portable communicator on her collar. 'Quarks are off the chart... We've found her.' She'd hit the jackpot as she'd identified the space-time signature which had been left behind by Tala's shiftband. A trail of quarks through space-time, like a trail of breadcrumbs in a forest.

The communicator buzzed and a husky male voice boomed in reply. 'Keep going,' he said. 'It won't be long before we lose her for good.'

Lera looked out to see her counterpart, Oskar Sykes, as he traversed several jagged rocks on the opposite side of the beach.

'Meet you halfway,' Sykes said over the comm.

'Affirmative,' Lera replied, as she quickened her pace. She observed the data from her V-Dis, and watched as the holographic readings changed depending on her direction of travel: increasing as a higher concentration of quarks were detected, and falling away when she moved too far from the trail.

They eventually met on a sloped bank. Lera studied the history of the region while Sykes finished his final scan of the beach. He was also dressed in line with the Company's strict requirements: slate cargo pants and a black fitted vest, which was pulled tightly over his toned torso. He had short-cropped hair and he was covered in tattoos. He had so many, in fact, that his nickname within the Company was 'Viper' in reference to the one most visible of them all: a snake which covered half of his chest, its open fangs visible above his collar.

'This way,' Lera said.

'You sure...? Scan says there's a higher concentration of quarks this way,' Sykes said, as he gestured towards the water's edge, where the waves crashed onto the beach. 'There was definitely some activity over there.'

'No Corporal,' said Lera. 'I've already found her signature. It's this way.'

Sykes glared at Lera until she looked away. He used his scanner to double-check Lera's results, then nodded. 'Looks like you're right, Tox... The path's lit up like a Christmas tree.'

Sykes wouldn't normally allow a new recruit to outdo him in this way, especially one only half his age. But as they happened to be alone, and as no one was there for him to show off to, he allowed the challenge to pass. Sykes had been impressed by Lera so far, especially when he considered how she'd only worked for the Company for less than a year. He'd already assessed that he'd only witnessed a fraction of what she was capable of. At eighteen, Lera had moved through the ranks faster than any of the Hunters he had known. She was strong-willed and intelligent, and Sykes respected her. 'Lead the way,' he said.

After following the trail of quarks for ten minutes or so, Sykes noticed the data had peaked to maximum levels. 'Hey, this is interesting,' he said, as he pointed to the treeline. 'Something's not right. It looks like there are two trails.'

'It must be a malfunction, surely,' Lera said, as she checked her own results. 'Maybe we need to reboot.'

'Nah. This trail's new. I say we check it out,' said Sykes. Lera agreed, and the pair edged their way through the undergrowth.

The Hunters' devices were not only optimised for tracking the number of quarks in a particular place, which indicated if a wormhole had opened or not, but they also calculated the approximate time when the wormhole was activated. The higher the concentration of quarks, the more recent the wormhole. As time passed, the concentration of quarks would be reduced, until eventually they would disappear altogether. At that point the trail would be virtually undetectable, and indistinguishable from the normal background levels of photons and quarks that bounced around the universe freely.

৳ Ⓗ β ঌ

And that, Lera pondered, would be a terrible outcome for Commander Tala, and an even more terrible outcome for her squadron: namely Lera and Sykes. Engella had slipped away too many times before, and Lera would not allow her to get away again. She thought back to her last conversation with Tala, who was so eager to follow Engella's trail that she had breached the Company's policy of never splitting away from the squadron. Since Tala had gone offline, Lera was becoming increasingly concerned. The sooner she found her, the better for everyone involved.

After a few minutes, the trail had gone cold again. Sykes began to swear, and grabbed at the trees until he ripped away several branches and twigs, his anger bubbling to the surface. 'What the hell is going on?' he said, his face sour.

'It's a false alarm,' said Lera. 'Trail's gone. We should go back the other —' Before she could finish, there was an explosion in the distance.

'Quick! This way!' Sykes said as he led them towards the noise, deep into the woods. They eventually noticed a clearing ahead, the echo of the blast still reverberating through the trees. Sunlight flashed through the canopy, and the air was filled with dust and smoke.

Sykes used a pair of binoculars and located a white cottage hidden among the trees. At first, it appeared as though the front door was wide open, but after further observation he realised that it wasn't open at all. The door had been completely blown away. In fact, part of the wall was missing too. The pair continued through the foliage and no longer spoke, using only hand signals to communicate.

'Something went down, here,' Sykes whispered. They waited to survey the cottage for any movement, but there was nothing – except for the clatter of the external shutters in the wind.

They rushed between the trees until they reached the gardens surrounding the cottage, concealing themselves as much as possible, and waited in silence before they decided upon their next move. As they edged along the pathway they both retrieved their blasters from their holsters.

Sykes pushed the gate but it creaked too much, so he released the pressure and held back. A second passed and he signalled to Lera to circle the cottage in one direction, while he went the other way. He reached the nearest window and peered through to check for anyone inside.

'Clear,' Sykes said, his whisper hardly making a

sound. After assessing it was safe to move forwards, Lera tiptoed through the rubble and charred wood, and stepped inside the doorway, her blaster primed and ready.

Indeed, something had gone on there. The scene was one of complete destruction. The explosion – most probably a shock-grenade – had destroyed most of the kitchen. Lera's eyes were drawn to a glimpse of yellow amongst the rubble. It wasn't long before she recognised it to be a piece of cable, the type used by the Company to secure prisoners. Lera then noticed a body laid across the middle of the cobbled floor, its clothes charred from blaster fire.

'No!' Lera yelled, as she ran to her commander's side, grabbing her wrist to check her pulse. It was weak, but she was still alive. 'I'll deal with Tala, you check the rest of the cottage.'

Sykes nodded and raced up the stairs with his blaster raised, while Lera rummaged inside her ruck-sack. She pulled out a medikit and reached inside to remove a small black sphere. She held it over Tala's chest and within seconds it had activated, hovering in place. A red light blinked, and then a narrow beam of light scanned Tala's still body. A holographic projection of her internal organs appeared, and displayed which organs required the most urgent attention. Her vital signs flashed in red, indicating she had suffered severe internal trauma.

Sykes returned to the ground floor. 'All clear,' he said.

'It looks like she has internal bleeding,' Lera said. 'She'll need surgery.' She reached inside her pocket and pulled out a transmitter which she fixed to the commander's lapel before she activated the comm.

'We've found Commander Tala,' Lera said.

A female voice boomed over the device. 'Is she alive?'

'Yes,' said Lera. 'But only just. I'm sending you our coordinates... Activating tracker ...' She waved her hand over the small sensor on Tala's cloak. 'Now.'

The comm buzzed before the voice returned. 'We've got her,' the woman said.

Almost instantly, lights flickered and space-time warped. A wormhole fissure appeared, and Commander Tala quickly disappeared through the vortex.

'You should have her,' Lera said.

'Affirmative, she's already in the medical bay.'

Lera breathed a sigh of relief. 'We'll finish up here,' she said. 'We're going after her.'

'Make sure you get her this time,' the woman said. 'For Tala's sake.'

Lera switched off the comm and paced the room,

not quite sure what their next move should be.

Sykes lifted a piece of rubble to reveal the body of a dog laid on its side. 'Someone lived here,' he said. 'We were close, this time. I think we only missed her by a few minutes.'

Lera paced across the kitchen, biting her nails as a rush of anxiety flowed over her like a waterfall.

'Get it together, recruit!' Sykes snapped, not giving a damn that Lera needed a moment to compose herself. She couldn't help but feel that if she had persuaded the commander to follow protocol, they probably would have had the criminal in custody by now, and Tala wouldn't be undergoing life-saving surgery in a medical bay.

Commander Tala had always watched out for Lera Mikias, ever since she'd joined the Company as a recruit the year before. Tala had been so impressed with Lera's abilities she was the one who'd given her the codename, Tox, when she began to move up the ranks. Tala had been impressed with the speed at which Lera was able to track down criminals and secure them as prisoners. She had joked that she'd never met a Hunter who was so toxic. Toxic later became Tox, for short. But none of that mattered now. Lera had to take full responsibility for what had occurred that day. She'd let the commander down, and she needed to make it right again. She wouldn't let an oversight like this happen again. She'd do everything she could to get the criminal responsible for injuring Tala, and she'd make her pay for her crimes.

By now, Sykes had continued his scan. 'I've got her,' he said. 'Here, in the centre of the room. Quarks are spiking. Wait... Yeah. Highest level we've seen for miles.'

'Wait a minute,' Lera said, as she examined the floor. 'Look at this.' She reached over and picked up the broken remains of a shiftband.

'Sykes, check its signature and compare it against the one from the beach,' Lera said.

Sykes worked quickly, analysing the shiftband's unique signature. 'How did you know?' he asked, his mouth open. 'They're different.'

Lera rubbed her hands together, before she activated the comm again. 'We have another problem,' she said. 'Check out this signature and run it through the database. It looks like Engella had help here.'

Within a few seconds, they had all the data they needed. The woman's voice buzzed over the comm again. 'Got it. Yeah, you're right. This signature's new. We've never seen it before.'

'I knew it!' Lera said, as she smashed her hand into her fist. She gestured to Sykes to prepare for them to leave. 'We'll need a clean-up crew here. There's damage which needs to be repaired. Plus this tech needs to be destroyed,' she said, referring to the damaged shiftband.

It wasn't long before a team of Hunters materialised beside them. They wore yellow protective suits, their faces concealed behind black goggles and gasmasks which covered their faces. They carried equipment on their backs which was connected to corrugated exhaust pipes, snaking around them like vines.

They began their work, directing beams of light at the damaged materials like firemen hosing water on a building. But instead of putting out flames, the beams had the effect of correcting any damage which had occurred. The table, which had been knocked on its side, suddenly stood up straight, while a chair which had been smashed in two was glued securely together again. The damaged cottage was as good as new, as if a wizard had cast a spell. But this was not magic. The device had in fact shifted the broken furniture back in time, to the moment before it had been destroyed, hence repairing the timeline in the process. The cottage was now perfectly tidy, except for one glaring omission. The only evidence of what had gone on there was the still body of a Labrador. Unfortunately, the technology had its limits.

Once the crew had finished, they shifted away one by one.

'We have Engella's coordinates,' Sykes said to Lera, who had completed his inspection of the clean-up crew's work. He activated his shiftband and a wormhole formed beside them. A strong breeze picked up from the other side, and dust and sand blew into the cottage around their feet. Lera peered through to see a vivid blue cloudless sky and a sandy desert. 'Let's find her,' she said, as they both stepped through.

A whirlwind of lights flickered and faded, and then the last remaining light went out, until the cottage was silent again. It was so still and silent, in fact, it was as though nothing had happened there at all.

β ଧ

2016-JUL-05 19:27

TRUTH OR CONSEQUENCES,

NEW MEXICO, UNITED STATES OF AMERICA

As he rested his head in his hands, Eduardo Reyes watched the patterns of sunlight as they formed on the slopes of Turtleback Mountain. He was supposed to be sweeping but he paused, just for a minute, for a well-deserved rest. The desert was silent except for the occasional howl of a coyote from deep inside the dusk. The stars began to appear, and the warm summer air cooled. A breeze picked up and Eddie was reminded it was time to get back to work.

He gripped the broom and brushed the dust and sand from the porch. Eddie and his mom had their daily routine, which they'd followed for as long as he could remember.

Maria would close down the restaurant for the night, waiting for the last customers to finish their food. She'd say her goodbyes, clear away the plates and prepare for the next day, before finally locking the glass doors as she left Maria's Restaurant and Motel for the night. Eddie, however, would tidy the house which sat on the opposite side of Highway 181, a few minutes' walk away, in preparation for his mom's return home. He'd empty the trash before meeting her in the kitchen where they'd prepare their evening meal together. They'd talk about their day over dinner, as they shared the left-over food from the restaurant. 'Waste not, want not,' Maria would say.

Eddie salivated as he thought about the pecan pie which had been freshly baked that morning. He had already decided the pie had his name all over it. He yawned and turned to the hammock which hung between the two main wooden posts on either side of the porch. He dived in, disappearing briefly into a pile of cushions. Eventually, the swing of the hammock slowed and Eddie noticed the temperature had dropped considerably. He shivered, pulling a chequered blanket over her legs, and made sure to tuck himself in. He placed his hands under his head, satisfied now he'd finally finished his chores. To

Eddie, dusk was the best part of the day. He loved the peace and quiet of the desert, and the way the light changed as the sun set: the silhouette of the mountain changing from a light grey to a deep purple.

Soda bubbled out as Eddie lifted the pull-tab of the can he'd placed outside in preparation. He removed the rest of the tab, sending little drops of the soda spitting everywhere. He gulped a mouthful and let out a sigh. Satisfied, his day was now complete.

After opening the camera app on his brand-new smartphone, which Maria had given him on his thirteenth birthday, he used the screen to check his image. The screen was filled with his big brown eyes, and he realised he was holding it a little too close. After adjusting his reach, his face was perfectly framed. He inspected his curly black hair and made sure his curls were still neatly placed, just as he liked them.

He flicked through the photographs stored on his phone until he reached the picture he was looking for: a falcon pair nesting with their chicks. He had taken this particular shot during a hiking trip in the nearby nature reserve. He was incredibly proud to have taken such a high-quality image, especially as he'd only used a smartphone. His photographs were improving with every hike. This had been the photo opportunity he'd been waiting for, definitely good enough to upload to his various social media accounts, and perhaps even good enough to submit to a wildlife competition.

A flash in the distance caught his attention. The sky was clear and the stars were out in force.

'There you are again,' he said. 'I'll get you this time.' This was not the first time he'd noticed the lights. They had appeared regularly over the last few months, flickering across the mountainside. He rummaged through his rucksack until he pulled out a pair of binoculars. By the time he had returned his gaze, the lights were gone.

Eddie surveyed the sky for any sign of a cloud, but there were none. In fact, the sky was perfectly clear. He had no idea where the lights were coming from.

He waited and watched, and he thought he'd missed his chance. 'Come on,' he said. 'Where have you gone?'

He was about to turn away, but a glint of light caught his eye.

'No way!' Eddie yelled.

The lights were back. And this time, he was looking directly at them. Surprised at his luck, he raced to the edge of the porch. Two streaks of white danced across the horizon, and then, just as suddenly as they appeared, they warped and merged into a single orb of emerald light which, blinking, returned just as suddenly.

'What the hell?' Eddie said, as he grabbed his phone from his pocket. He flicked through to the camera app and tried to use the zoom function to focus the image.

The lights were now as clear as day, but by the time he'd managed to prepare the shot, they'd flickered out again.

Absolutely nothing remained. Only the black of night.

'Ah man,' Eddie said, as he kicked his foot against the steps.

The outer door clapped against the porch, startling the boy.

'Hey, Eddie, I'm home,' Maria said, as she pushed her way through the front door. She was holding a brown paper bag – which looked as though it may split at any moment – full to the brim with groceries.

'Hey, Mom.'

Maria placed the bag on the kitchen counter and joined her son on the porch. 'How was your day?' she asked.

'Good,' Eddie replied. 'School was okay, but I can't wait for summer break. I want to get back to the nature reserve. Those chicks won't be in the nest for much longer.'

'Ah, yes the nature reserve,' Maria said. 'About that...' She didn't have time to finish, as Eddie interrupted, excited to share his news.

'I saw the lights again,' he said.

'You did? Now, come on Eddie. Enough of the UFOs, okay? You need to focus on your math. You have a test coming up soon.'

'I know, Mom,' he said, letting out a sigh. He wandered over to the counter and was about to peer inside the grocery bag, secretly hoping to find the pecan pie waiting for him. 'What are we eating?' he said.

'Do we have a feast tonight!' Maria said, grabbing the bag from Eddie, before he had the chance to look inside.

Eddie was the image of his mother, their big brown eyes so similar that not a day passed when they didn't receive a comment about it. Everyone who ever met them almost certainly knew that they were mother and son.

Maria grabbed Eddie and pulled him close, hugging him tightly.

'Mom!' Eddie yelled as he tried to pull away, but grinning from ear to ear.

Maria opened up the bag and pulled out some cardboard containers. 'We've got a couple of steaks, lots of salad, and the best thing of all... A *big* piece of pecan pie each for dessert!'

Eddie smiled. 'Sounds great, Mom.'

'I'm just going to get into something more comfortable. Give me twenty minutes or so and I'll serve dinner. It's still warm outside. How about we eat on the porch? We may as well enjoy the weather while it lasts. It'll be getting chilly in the evenings again before we know it.'

Eddie nodded. 'Sure thing,' he said.

'But, honey, I need to tell you something first. It's about the nature reserve... I didn't get time for a break today, as the restaurant was just so busy. I was chatting to this guy who works in Albuquerque, and he said the old military base near the State Park has been sold off. Apparently, they're completely refitting the place. He works for this big company that's paying for the whole thing. The problem is, they've made the exclusion zone around the facility twice as large than it was before. I'm sorry, hon, but they're going to take over most of the reserve.'

'They can't do that! It's protected!' Eddie yelled.

'I know, son. It's terrible,' Maria said, frowning. 'I

don't know how the hell they get away with it. But you know how it works with these big companies. All they need to do is send over the big bucks and they get their way.'

'They can't do that! Surely? Can they really stop us going in there?!'

Eddie thought about his weekend hikes, and he couldn't imagine what life would be like without them.

'And what about the animals there? Will they still be protected?'

'I don't know, Eddie. If the guy at the restaurant was right and they've sold off the land, it's private property now. They can do whatever they like with it, unfortunately.'

Eddie shook his head. 'Not cool,' he said.

'I'm sorry. I know that place means a lot to you but it's going to be a while yet, so I don't think we should worry about it for now. Let me go change and I'll get this feast going. Okay?'

'Okay, Mom.'

Maria went back inside, leaving Eddie to contemplate the news. As he looked out towards the mountain, he grumbled to himself. The only lights which he could see now, were the stars of the constellations *Ursa Major* and *Ursa Minor*, which shone brightly above.

'What are you?' he asked, as he thought about the strange lights. He shook his head, left the porch, and followed his mom inside.

If only he'd stayed for another few seconds.

This time, the lights appeared in the same spot as before, and glared like the sun at noon. Glowing orbs of yellow and flashes of white flickered across the base of Turtleback Mountain, like two dancers in an embrace.

The incredible show of lights almost lasted a whole minute, this time around.

Far longer than ever before.

2016-JUL-05 19:55
TURTLEBACK MOUNTAIN,
OUTSIDE TRUTH OR CONSEQUENCES,
NEW MEXICO, UNITED STATES OF AMERICA

'There's another one,' said Annys, as she pointed towards the mountaintop. A succession of shooting stars streaked across the sky. Annys had discovered what had turned out to be the perfect vantage point on the hillside, a plot of land nestled beside Turtleback Mountain which had panoramic views of the valley. They could see a town in the distance and the expanse of the desert, which was framed by a starry sky.

'Wow, they're beautiful,' Engella said, her eyes transfixed. Annys glanced at her portable computer, waiting patiently while data about their surroundings streamed in. A few seconds passed and the system chimed.

Annys smiled to herself before turning to face Engella. 'Yes, here we go,' she said. 'I've been checking the coordinates I was provided with, and I think this is the right place.' She'd planned their arrival with almost perfect accuracy, and she was content in the knowledge that their location in space-time was the one they'd been looking for, although it had taken them several shifts to find the correct point in time.

Shifting through space-time required two elements: accurate spatial coordinates and a precise calculation of the timepoint too. Without both pieces of data, the person who was shifting could find themselves at the correct place, but could be there either too early or too late. In fact, they could find themselves out by days, months or even years.

'I see,' said Engella, as she pondered this for a moment. 'So, what's the plan again?' she asked.

Annys had already explained why they'd travelled to this particular location in space-time, but she was happy to summarise the key points of their plan again. 'First, we need to check the surrounding area, and we'll need to collect intelligence on the compound down there. It'll be a Hunter base, one day.'

'If you already know there will be a Hunter base here, why does it matter when they set it up?' Engella asked, confused.

'We have people counting on us to collect some vital information,' Annys said, looking away. 'If our intelligence is correct, and I believe it is, the place down there – the old military base – will one day become the central hub of the Hunters' operations.'

Engella gazed out at the desert below. 'Ah, yes, I can see it,' she said. 'It doesn't look like much at the moment, except for those guard towers, they look rather threatening.'

'No, it doesn't look like anything yet. But one day it will be a very important place for the Hunters. And that makes it very important to us. If we're able to work out exactly when they'll arrive here, we may be able to help a lot of innocent people.'

Engella nodded, but she still didn't quite understand how collecting information on an old airbase could be so important. Still, she trusted Annys's reasoning, so she felt it was important not to raise the matter again.

Annys was about to speak but she turned, just in time, to see Engella leap up – her eyes wide with excitement.

'Look, there's another one!' Engella said, as a spark of light painted the sky.

'Fantastic! There's definitely something to be said about time travel, you get to experience some great moments. When we're finished, with our mission, I mean, I'll take you to see one of the greatest meteor showers in history. Those shooting stars will look like fireflies in comparison.'

'Sounds great,' said Engella, but her expression changed, turning sombre. 'But, about our mission...'

'Yes?'

'I'm happy to help you get the information you need, but I'll need to get back to New Shanghai soon after. I was searching for information about the whereabouts of my parents, but the Hunters got on my tail. I was close to finding something, I just know it. I need to go back.'

'We won't need to be here long,' Annys said. She looked away, as if she didn't know what else to say.

'I'm still not clear why you're helping me,' said Engella. 'I'm so confused about everything that has happened over the last few days.'

'All I can say, dear, is that you shouldn't worry about any of this for now. We have a few important tasks to complete first. After we've done the things we need to do, everything will be much clearer, I promise.'

Engella nodded, satisfied that she could put her faith in Annys.

'Right, dear, I think it's time we set up camp,' Annys said with a wink. 'I'm afraid you're responsible for tent duty again today.'

'Not again... Do I have to?' Engella asked, her grin wide. She sighed and chuckled to herself. 'Oh, okay, if I must.' She pulled out a tiny reflective cube from her pocket and flicked it into the air. 'Activate,' she said.

The cube expanded rapidly into a large black tent, and flopped onto the sand with a thump, leaving a tiny halo of sand drifting on the wind.

'Good work,' Annys said, chuckling. 'Now, why don't I get the fire going while you set up the perimeter?'

Engella had been relieved when she'd learned about the preparations which Annys had made for their journey. She'd packed a large bag of supplies before Engella had even arrived at the cottage, ready and waiting in case of an urgent getaway. The rucksack was packed with a few pieces of warm clothing, several packets of food tablets and a variety of helpful devices and camping equipment, such as the cube-tent.

After spending several months living on the streets, Engella was grateful to finally have somewhere warm and dry to sleep. The cube-tent was like a luxurious palace compared to the streets of New Shanghai.

Annys wandered through the dry thicket and tumbleweeds surrounding their campsite, primarily to assess the access routes, but also to collect data on the composition of the rocks. Engella, meanwhile, had been tasked with security, and she'd placed three proximity sensors at equal distances around the camp – stationed in the shape of a triangle.

Engella removed a Tri-Key from her utility belt – a small triangular device which was an absolute must for any serious camper, or anyone else, for that matter, who didn't have access to regular cooking facilities. Once activated the device glowed, first orange and then a sunflower-yellow, as it began to radiate heat. It was perfect for their needs, as it provided just enough heat to cook the food tablets while generating enough additional heat to keep them warm too. It wasn't long before the Tri-Key glowed a vivid white.

'It's time, Engella,' Annys said. 'We don't want anyone spotting us while we're up here.' Even though the Tri-Key was a stealthier mode of cooking than using a campfire, there was still the slim chance that the glow would be visible from the town below.

Engella agreed, and picked up the V-Dis, another

one of the devices that Annys had packed among their supplies. She switched off the holographic display to save power, but also to limit the amount of light that was emitted, which could potentially give away their location on the hillside. It was important to avoid any unwanted attention, after all. She tapped the screen and watched as the three sensors lit up, one after the other.

A shimmer swam across the camp. The energy wave from the sensors had adjusted the image frequency just enough for the camp to become completely reflective, so it took on the appearance of the hillside. They were now completely hidden, protected by an invisible cloak.

Engella placed a picnic blanket on the ground and sat down, her legs crossed, while Annys searched for something for them to eat. After several minutes of rummaging through their rations, she eventually found what she had been looking for: two small tablets; one shaped like a slice of pizza and the other like a piece of sushi.

'What are we eating tonight?' Engella asked, hopefully.

'Food's low,' Annys said. 'We'll need to stop for supplies soon.'

α β γ

'I suggest we shift into the future soon, so we can stock up on these. What do you think?'

'Yes, definitely!' Engella said, as she saw what Annys was holding in her hand. 'They're my favourite!'

'Mine too,' said Annys.

The small tablets didn't look like much, but this could be misleading, and as Annys would always say, 'Never judge a book by its cover.' Food tablets were similar in style to the freeze-dried foods which had been used by astronauts in the twentieth century. But unlike freeze-dried foods, however, food tablets were particularly unique in that the food was not only rehydrated, but most of the textures and tastes were generated by invisible tiny robots called nanobots. Once activated the tablets were almost identical to the real, freshly cooked food which they were based upon.

Annys smiled at Engella. 'What will it be tonight then? Pizza or sushi?'

'Let me think ... Pizza, without a doubt!' Engella said, excited at the prospect.

'Pizza it is,' Annys replied, placing the pizza-shaped food tablet on top of the glowing Tri-Key.

The food tablet began to warm, its texture changing from a crisp-white powder to a globular mass, before it expanded outwards suddenly in a flop of dough and cheese. Soon it was ready and a bubbling pizza rested in its place, with droves of melted cheese dripping over the edges of the Tri-Key like lava.

Annys waited for the cheese to cool. 'Dinner's ready,' she said. 'Let's tuck in.'

Engella sliced the pizza into equal pieces and passed Annys a slice. The cheese was warm and delicious, and Engella couldn't help but lick her lips while she ate.

'Not quite as good as my apple pie, dear, but I have to say. This is not that bad at all,' Annys said.

They ate their meal quickly, not saying a word until they'd almost finished, although, the silence unsettled Annys. She'd noticed a change in Engella's mood, who now had a sombre look about her. Something was clearly on her mind.

Annys waited for Engella to finish her last bite of pizza before speaking. 'Is everything okay, dear? How are you feeling?' she asked.

Engella hesitated and looked down at the ground, not wishing to look at Annys directly. 'Yes, I'm okay, I think,' she said, before pausing again as she considered her next words carefully. 'It's just ... I don't know. I think I'm still a little jumpy after what happened in the cottage.' It had now been over a week since the events in Skye, and Engella hadn't had a good night's sleep since.

Annys shuffled closer and placed her hand on Engella's shoulder. 'I thought so. I knew something was up. It'll take some time, dear. You've been through a lot. It's inevitable you'd be affected.'

Engella continued. 'I've had close calls before. Some have been worse than others, believe me. But this time felt different. I thought that was it, I really did.'

'But it wasn't, dear. You're here with me, now. You're safe, I promise.'

Engella shook her head. 'Thanks, Annys. I get it, I really do. But for how long? I'm so tired of running,' she said, looking down. She started to speak again, but paused.

'What is it, dear?'

'Something just doesn't add up. There's something which is still bothering me.'

'Go on.'

'It was the Hunter, the one who chased me from New Shanghai to the cottage. She was different, I mean, there was something about her which frightened me. She had so much anger towards me. I just don't understand why.'

'You've been on the run for a long time,' said Annys. 'I guess they're starting to take it personally now. I'd try not to think about it, if I were you.'

Engella looked into Annys's eyes. Her face had a warm glow about it, lit up by the Tri-Key.

'They'll never stop, will they?'

This time, it was Annys who looked away. 'It's getting cold,' Annys said, as she pulled out a blanket. 'How's this?' she said, as she placed it over Engella's legs.

'Good, thank you.'

Engella was about to say something, but she held back.

'What is it?' said Annys. 'It's okay. What's on your mind?'

'You haven't really told me much. About ... well anything, really. Apart from the mission, of course. I'm still very confused.'

Annys paused, taken aback by the directness of Engella's question. She placed her finger on her lip and nibbled her fingernail. Engella had noticed Annys did this when she was contemplating her next move. The last time she had seen her do it was when they were in the cottage together, before their escape. A moment passed, and then Annys's shrewd look turned to one of concern.

Engella sat up, eager to listen to her reply. 'Well?' she asked.

Annys hesitated. 'I-I ...' she said, stuttering.

'Yes?' Engella's change of tone made Annys's cheeks flush.

'There are rules, dear,' Annys said.' I'm not able to say too much. The future depends on it.'

'The future?' Engella asked. 'What about now?'

'We're now part of a series of events which have already been set in motion. I can't tell you every-thing, as by telling you about certain facts may impact them, perhaps even changing them forever. The events, I mean.'

'In what way can we change them?'

'Well, it could change the order of events, or even the timing of when they're going to happen. Or, per-haps, it could change things so much that the events that are supposed to happen never happen at all.'

Engella listened intently. 'Go on,' she said.

Annys nodded, her posture now more relaxed. 'Have you heard of the butterfly effect?' she asked.

'Yes, I have,' Engella said. 'My father theorised about it, as part of his research.' Her tone changed to one of sadness, as she thought of him.

'Yes, that's right,' said Annys. 'I believe it's part of what is known as chaos theory. The butterfly effect states that an insignificant change in one place can have dramatic consequences elsewhere.'

'Papa explained it to me once. He said to imagine a butterfly flapping its wings. The flapping causes a tiny breeze, which slowly increases in strength as it moves across the field. Eventually, the breeze turns into a gust, which creates a storm, until finally, it becomes a hurricane that destroys a city on the other side of the world... Scary, eh?'

'Yes, that's exactly it,' said Annys. 'I'm sure you can understand how this is incredibly relevant to space-time travel. Let's pretend I told you to cross the road at a certain time tomorrow. I give you the exact time and place of where to cross, in the knowledge that you'll be safe to meet me on the other side. Perhaps we're supposed to leave through a wormhole at that exact place and time. What would happen if you decided to change the time, let's say, by a few minutes? What happens when you cross the road, five minutes later than the time we had agreed? What about if a bus drives through when you're crossing? Imagine if you were injured? You wouldn't be able to make the meeting point on time. It could change everything.'

'Yes, I understand,' said Engella.

'Everything must happen as it's meant to happen. It's very important.'

'What do you mean? Why's it so important? I'm

sick of the riddles, Annys. We can change whatever we want, surely. I want to change things.' Engella said, her eyes welling up. 'I want to find my parents, that's all I care about.'

Annys nodded. 'I know you miss them, dear. But we need to accept things as they are.'

Engella shook her head. 'I want to go back to how everything used to be.'

'I'm sorry, dear. Really, I am. I want to tell you more, but I need to be careful. I can't say too much, it's really that important. But I'll try to answer your questions, if I can.'

Engella accepted this, and nodded. She determined that some knowledge was better than no knowledge at all.

'Okay. Tell me when to stop – if I go too far, that is,' Engella said.

Annys agreed. 'What would you like to know?' she said, pensively.

'First of all, who exactly are you?'

'I'm a friend... That's all I can say for now.'

'Okay... If you can't tell me more about yourself, who do you work for?'

'I can tell you one thing, dear. I only have your best interests at heart. We all do. I'm here for you always, I promise. My friends and I care very deeply about you. Your protection is our top priority, no matter what.'

Even though Engella was still none the wiser, she considered the words carefully, and there was one thing she felt sure about: she was right to trust her intuition. Even when nothing else made sense, she had been right to trust Annys.

'What do you know about the Company?' asked Engella.

'Very little, but enough for us to stay one step ahead,' said Annys. 'We've been able to piece together information about it over the years. It's called the Huntington Corporation.'

'Hence, the Hunters,' said Engella.

'Yes, to a degree, but the Hunters you know are not the Company as such. They're a dangerous group of thugs whom the Company employs to do its dirty work. But I think even the best agencies, you know, the police or the secret service, wouldn't be able to link the Hunters to the Company. The corporation is just too big and powerful.'

The Huntington Corporation was created in the mid-2050s and quickly rose to become the largest tech company in the world – making billions of credits in the process. The Company's first taste of success came when it created the first sentient Artificial Intelligence and placed it in the body of an android. The surge in profits it received enabled it to move into additional technology development, including inter-spatial-time-travel. Its initial goal was to use the technology to fix the problems of the past. Yet it wasn't long before it started using the technology for its own gains. After several minor indiscretions related to lottery fraud, the Company's strategies became far more insidious. Its original intention to change the world for the better was soon replaced with an insatiable hunger to gain more and more profits for its shareholders.

'What kind of dirty work?' asked Engella.

'You know, anything illegal. It started with lottery fraud, for example – shifting through space-time to find out which numbers would be drawn and getting rich in the process. I believe it increased its profits by billions with this method alone. Fraudulently, of course. And anyone who didn't agree with its methods would suffer, or be silenced. The Company's criminal activities increased as its profits soared, until it went as far as, well … hurting people – being sure to get rid of anyone who got in its way. Or, perhaps, anyone who no longer supported its interests.'

'Like my parents.'

'Yes, dear. I know your parents worked for the Company in the early days, and that they joined in good faith. Unfortunately, they had no idea what they were getting themselves into – until it was too late. Your parents needed funding for their research, and the Company came along with an offer they just couldn't refuse. But it wasn't long before their relationship deteriorated. The Company quickly recognised the huge potential of shiftband technology and the power they could attain by controlling it. Profit and power became more important than people, I assume.'

'So why are the Hunters after me?'

'Your knowledge. They think you know where the other shiftbands are.'

'Shiftbands?'

Annys pointed to her wristband.

'That's the name your parents gave to them after they had developed the technology and created the prototypes.'

'How do you have one? I thought I had the only one.'

'Somebody close gave it to me. Your parents created five prototypes. I believe it was your father who first suspected that the Company planned to take their research by force, so your mother hid the other four shiftbands, taking only one for themselves.'

'So, they gave me the only one they had,' said Engella, her eyes welling up.

'Yes, dear. The Hunters won't stop until they've found them, or until they're destroyed. I don't think they care either way... They copied the technology from your parents' research, but they don't want anyone else to have the ability to shift. That means they need to find and destroy the prototypes, so only the Company has the ability to travel through space-time. They want to keep the technology under their control. We're in the way, Engella. Until they get rid of all traces of us, they'll never stop.'

Engella considered what she had learned. 'If they destroy all of the shiftbands, I'll never find my parents,' she said. The Hunters had been hellbent on capturing her. She'd never understood why, yet it all started to make sense now, except for one point which still didn't quite add up. 'But if my parents only had one wristband, erm ... shiftband, which they gave to me, how do you have one? I thought you said the other four were hidden.'

'That's right...' Annys said. 'There are four shift-bands left, including mine. We need to find the others before the Hunters get to them. All of our futures depend on it, Engella. I have an idea as to where we can find them, but it's just a hunch at the moment.'

Engella finally found the courage to ask the question she'd wanted to ask all along. 'I have one more question...' she said, although, if she was completely honest with herself, she already knew the answer. 'Do you know where my parents are?'

'I'm sorry, Engella. I don't,' said Annys. 'Why don't you tell me what you remember about the day you lost them? If you want to, of course.'

'It's so long ago,' Engella said. 'But I still remember it like it was yesterday.'

'Think back. How old were you? Where did it happen? Any details may help us understand what happened to them.'

Engella closed her eyes and thought about that fateful day, which had been forever etched into her mind. 'I remember we were surrounded. Wormholes appeared all around us and there were Hunters everywhere. They managed to find our location in space-time, and they hit us with everything they had. It was a coordinated assault. Whichever way we turned, they were there. We didn't stand a chance. Papa put his wristband on me, I mean, shiftband, and before I knew it, I'd been pushed through the nearest portal. I didn't even know what had happened, until it was too late.'

Engella's voice was shaky, but she managed to hold back the tears.

'I know it's hard for you dear, but it's very important. If your parents were left behind, it's likely they were captured.'

'I thought so too, but they made it out, I know they did.'

'When was this?' asked Annys.

'I was eight. I've been on my own ever since, fending for myself.' At that moment, Engella realised she'd been separated from her parents for longer than she'd ever known them. It was a sad fact, and something which was difficult to accept.

'I'm sorry, Engella, I really am,' said Annys. 'So, after you escaped, where did you end up next?'

'New Shanghai, initially. I waited for my parents, in case they were able to follow. I hoped Papa had sent me there for a reason. After a few months, I almost gave up, until I finally received a message from him. I knew he wouldn't leave me there alone. If it wasn't for the message, I honestly don't think I'd be here today. It gave me the hope I needed to carry on looking for them.'

Annys was now intrigued. 'What message?' she asked.

Engella reached inside her rucksack, and pulled out a small silver device – a holocube. The outer casing was weathered and scratched – the device had definitely seen better days. She passed it to Annys, who waved her hand over the activation panel. A hologram materialised above them, the lights flickering, illuminating the desert floor. Annys watched as a young girl wearing a blue-and-white-chequered dress skipped along a yellow-brick road. The holomovie was instantly recognisable.

'*The Wizard of Oz*,' Annys said, her grin wide.

'Look closer,' said Engella, who gestured towards the flickers of light.

The holographic Dorothy continued to skip, until she was joined by the Tin Man and the Scarecrow, two of the other lead characters from the holomovie. And then a strange thing happened. The three characters were joined by a fourth, yet something wasn't right with the character's appearance. Instead of a colourful image like the three other holo-characters, this one was only a shadow. It was as if their code had somehow been deleted from the device's memory bank.

The hologram flickered for a final time, before it began to replay from the start, the same images on repeat.

Engella deactivated the holocube then turned it

over, showing Annys the underside. 'It's a message,' she said. 'The hologram, I mean. But it's not just the hologram itself. There's also this too ... Look here ...'

Annys took the device and examined the words, and then read them aloud.

Keep going. We'll find you. ER.
α - β - γ - δ - ε

'Curious,' she said. 'These symbols are letters from the Greek alphabet.' She pondered this, and then continued. 'But, I think I know what they mean.'

'What are they?' Engella asked eagerly. She'd tried to understand the meaning of the symbols for so long. At last she was about to be one step closer to decoding the message she'd received from her father, all those years before.

'They're designations, codenames if you will...' Annys said. 'Look at this...' She pulled back her sleeve to reveal her shiftband, and pointed to a small symbol inscribed on the inside rim. It was the symbol 'β' – the Greek letter Beta, as Annys had just pointed out.

'This is odd, though,' Annys said, returning to the message on the holocube. 'Alpha has been crossed out...' She highlighted the Alpha symbol, noting it had been scribed through with a single line. 'I wonder why that is?'

'I don't know,' said Engella. 'But I am sure about one thing... This is a message from Papa.'

'How can you be sure?' asked Annys.

'ER,' said Engella. 'Dr Evan Rhys. He's sending me a message, I know it.'

Annys nodded, and allowed Engella to continue.

'Papa always signed off his emails with ER,' Engella said, smiling. 'Just like the Queen of England, he'd say... but I never really understood what that meant.'

'Evan Rhys. Yes, of course. From what I've heard about him, he was an incredible scientist.'

'He *is* an incredible scientist,' Engella said, not pleased by Annys's choice of words.

'Sorry, dear, of course. Didn't Evan win the Nobel Prize for Physics for his work on interspatial-time-travel?'

'Yes, he did,' said Engella.

'If my research is correct, I believe he shared the prize with Dr May Nakamura,' said Annys. 'Another outstanding scientist.'

'My mother.'

'You should be incredibly proud of their achievements,' Annys said, 'I wish I could have met them.

What was it that your mother discovered...? Don't tell me. She was the person who identified that it was theoretically possible to track quarks through space-time.'

'Yes, that's right. It was all over the news.'

'What was it they called it?' Annys asked, as she racked her brains, trying hard to remember. 'Ah yes, lights and time?'

Engella smirked. 'Almost,' she said. 'They named it The Lights of Time.'

'Yes! I remember now!' said Annys. 'It caused a real furore. I bet it went down a storm in the tabloids. The discovery of a generation. Being able to track events through space-time, and editing them just enough to improve the outcome – allowing us to change our pasts for a better future. Wonderful, in the right hands, of course. But fraught with dangers too... I don't know how it all ended like this...'

Engella found the trip down memory lane particularly difficult to digest. 'There are no records about any of this anymore. Only what we can remember,' she said. 'It's like everything they did, all of their achievements – even their Nobel prize – never happened. All evidence of their existence was deleted from the timeline. It's as if they had never existed at all. I started digging further over the years, checking any data I could find from the historical records, but there was nothing, not even a trace.'

'The Company damn well made sure nothing was left,' Annys said. 'That's how they work, I'm afraid.'

'Do you know the worst thing of all? It sounds silly when I say it aloud.'

'Go on, dear. You can tell me anything.'

'I don't even have a photograph of them... Sometimes I feel as though I'm going to forget what they looked like... It makes me so sad.'

'Have you heard from them since?' Annys asked. 'Since the holocube message, I mean?'

'No,' Engella said, bluntly. 'I never heard from them again.'

This time it was Annys who became upset, her eyes welling up. 'I'm sorry you lost your parents,' she said, as she rubbed her eyes. 'Gosh, dear, it's making me emotional just thinking about it. I can only imagine how hard it must have been for you.' She reached out and placed an arm around Engella's back. 'I'm sorry for everything you've been through.'

'It's okay,' Engella said. 'It's not your fault.'

Annys was about to return the holocube when something else caught her eye. 'Hold on,' she said.

'Look at this, here... It looks as if there's another projector, hidden inside this panel. It's tiny, but there's definitely something there.'

Engella examined the device carefully and Annys was right: the device did in fact have a second holographic projector hidden on the underside of the device, so tiny it was almost invisible to the naked eye. Engella couldn't believe she'd never noticed it before, and she was even more impressed with how Annys had spotted it so easily.

After tampering with the device for several minutes, the holographic image transformed into a much larger projection.

Engella gasped. 'I've never seen this before...' She examined the hologram, which continued to grow in size and intensity. 'I can't believe it!' she said.

'It looks like a map,' said Annys.

Engella agreed. 'You're right. And I've been here, many times in fact... It's New Shanghai.'

Engella waved her hand through the projection: the imagery expanding and shrinking depending on how she moved, closing in on the streets or zooming out to see the whole cityscape. A red light blinked on one of the upper levels of the city, and Engella zoomed in to the location of the light.

Annys read it aloud...

GRAVITON DYNAMICS
Where the past and future unite

EVERGREEN GARDENS,
NEW SHANGHAI CITY, ASIAN PROTECTORATE

'I know this place,' Annys said.

'You do?'

'Yes. This was your parents' research laboratory, well, until the takeover at least.'

'The takeover?'

'When the Huntington Corporation bought out your parents' business. They basically merged the research laboratory with another department they already owned.'

Engella nodded. 'Right, yes. This place, what's it called? Evergreen Gardens? That was near to the place where I was when I found the holocube.'

Engella moved the map to a position about ten blocks from the blinking light.

'Papa left it for me at this point,' she said. 'I think it means something, don't you? Perhaps the other shiftbands are around there?'

'Possibly, dear,' said Annys. 'But I would imagine your parents' offices would have been the first place they'd have looked.'

'Yes, I suppose,' said Engella. 'But I wonder what it means?'

Annys was about to reply when a small boulder tumbled down the hillside, which was followed quickly by a haze of dust. Engella turned off the holographic projection and returned the device to her rucksack, remaining as silent as possible.

'Stay here,' Annys whispered. She moved off, making as little sound as possible, to review the camp's perimeter. Yet there was nothing to be seen.

Annys reviewed the data on her V-Dis, in case there had been any wormhole activity. 'Quarks look fine,' she whispered. 'But I'm going to keep a look out anyway – just in case. It's better to be safe than sorry.'

'Okay,' Engella said.

Annys stopped pacing and finally settled down. 'I'll be fine keeping watch,' she said. 'I'm not tired, anyway. You, on the other hand dear, need to get some shut-eye. You're exhausted.' Although it was only early evening, they had discovered it was a good idea to sleep whenever they found the opportunity.

The change in time which inevitably occurred after space-time travel was always a shock to the system, especially for Engella, who was particularly sensitive. Moving between the same hour of the day on different days was not much of a problem, but moving from day to night, or vice versa, was particularly disorientating. Annys compared the feeling to that of jetlag. In fact, she'd named it shiftlag. Unfortunately, the more a person shifted through space-time the more their body clock would get out of sync, until eventually they were so tired they didn't know what was going on at all. The best remedy for shiftlag, Engella had determined, was to stay in one place for a few weeks and ideally for a month, giving her body the chance to settle before shifting again. Yet, this had its own challenges. The longer they stayed in one place, the more likely it would be that the Hunters would catch up with them.

For Engella, the effects of shiftlag had been getting far worse. These days, she'd get headaches and nausea every time she was anywhere near a wormhole, let alone travelling through one. In fact, she was now so sensitive to the changes in space-time that she was able to detect wormhole activity from miles away, even without the use of any technology.

'I don't think I'll be able to sleep,' said Engella. 'We need to go back to New Shanghai.'

'Try to sleep,' said Annys. 'We can think about our next move once you've rested.'

After some persuasion, Engella agreed, and rolled out her sleeping bag to prepare for rest. 'I'm going to stay up a little longer though,' she said. 'I need to make some notes in my journal.'

Annys smiled. 'Of course, dear.'

Engella spent the next half hour noting down everything she'd seen in the holocube projection, scribbling notes alongside, and circling the important points. She scrawled a question across the top of the page, in capital letters:

WHAT DOES THIS MEAN?

Her thoughts were racing, and she couldn't get the image of the map out of her mind. How had she missed this? She'd had the holocube for years.

Still, it didn't matter now – the problem she now faced was how she would be able persuade Annys to join her on a trip to New Shanghai. She was eager to go back there and explore the area in greater detail, but it would be dangerous – and Annys would surely reject her request. She'd need to find a way to get there. But that was a problem for another day. She tried to clear her mind, and settled into her warm sleeping bag. The zip was pulled right up to her chin and she was packed so tightly and snug inside, she could barely move.

She closed her eyes and rested, and it wasn't long before she had fallen fast asleep.

2016-JUL-05 19:55
TRUTH OR CONSEQUENCES,
NEW MEXICO, UNITED STATES OF AMERICA

They sat silently while the television blared in the background, its screen lighting the walls of the sitting room. Maria rested her head on a cushion, uninterested in the show they'd supposedly been watching. She played with the remote between her fingers and decided it was time to turn off for the night. She flicked the off switch and turned to her son, who was laid on his back staring at the ceiling.

'Come on, mister,' Maria said. 'It's time for you to do your homework... Before it gets too late.' She got up from the chair and began to tidy away the remains of dinner.

'Ah, Mom, do I have to?'

'Yes, honey, you do,' You have a test coming up. No excuses, okay?'

'Okay, Mom...' Eddie knew his mother wouldn't budge, however hard he tried – so he didn't even try.

'Let me make you a drink,' said Maria. 'How about a cup of cocoa?'

Eddie grinned. 'Oh, go on then,' he said. He picked up his rucksack and threw it over his shoulder before making his way to the back door. 'Can I at least do it outside, under the stars?'

'It's a deal,' said Maria, happy to reach a compromise.

Eddie acknowledged this with a thumbs-up, and went outside to clear a space on the porch. He reached inside his backpack and pulled out his note-book. The front cover was crammed with stickers of superheroes and American football stars, while the crisp white pages inside were hardly touched. It was obvious he rarely used it. After turning to the inside cover, he skimmed through the fractions, sums and algebra on the page, and pondered the first question. Unfortunately, he had no idea where to begin and it wasn't long before his face turned from anguish to frustration. He slammed the notebook shut, completely dismayed. 'I hate math,' he said.

By now, the twilight outside had faded to a pitch-black, the stars now the only lights visible. It was for this reason that what happened next was so very strange.

A cascade of lights twinkled on the horizon, somewhere in the approximate vicinity of the base of Turtleback Mountain.

Eddie knew instantly what was about to happen, as he had seen it time and time again. He grabbed his phone in anticipation, and raced down the steps, sending his notebook tumbling in the process.

'Wow!' he yelled, as he focused the zoom function on his camera app on the distant lights. His finger went into overdrive, clicking away, his brown eyes never leaving the incredible light show for a second. He didn't even slow to check the quality of the images – there would be time for that later. What mattered now was getting as many photographs as possible. He wasn't going to miss his chance. Not this time.

The lights began to fade, and when Eddie realised the lights had gone out again, he closed down the camera app and placed his smartphone in his pocket. The adrenaline rush had subsided and his breathing returned to normal, even though his heart was still racing. He rushed to the door and shouted through to Maria. 'Going out, Mom, I'll be back soon!' he yelled.

Maria barely had time to register, let alone tell him 'no'.

'Wait, Eddie?! What are you doing?!' she yelled.

'It's important!' Eddie said, as he ran down the steps. 'I'll be back soon, I promise.'

Maria shook her head, and hurried to dry her hands before sprinting to the back door, swinging it open with a clatter. By the time she had reached the porch, Eddie was already running into the night.

'You're crazy!' Maria yelled. Her gaze followed Eddie into the desert as he dashed towards Turtle-back Mountain.

Suddenly, a bright flash caught her eye. She gasped as she saw a series of sparkling lights dance across the hillside. Stunned, she watched them sparkle – her eyes transfixed by the wonder of it all.

She couldn't believe what she was seeing. Eddie had been right all along.

Q Q Q

Eddie observed the lights as they flashed erratically beside the mountain. As soon as he was able to track one, it disappeared. When he was about to give up, another one would emerge from the night, teasing him to continue the chase.

What are you? he thought.

The lights weren't like anything Eddie had seen before. He wondered what they could have been, ever since they'd first appeared a few months earlier. There were two plausible theories which he'd been able to narrow it down to: meteor showers and lightning. After thinking about it, however, he'd determined that meteors wouldn't fall so low to the horizon. They were always visible high in the sky, as they burnt up in the atmosphere. There was only one option left now: lightning, although, this would always originate from the top of the clouds, crackling to the Earth in a fork, or filling the whole sky with a bright flash.

These lights were different.

In fact, they were tiny pin-pricks of colour which always appeared in the same place, repeatedly, although they could sometimes be separated by weeks and even months. They were a variety of colours, but mostly hues of blue. Eddie had never seen coloured lightning before, although he was sure he'd read about it in a book once. Perhaps this was one of those special, rare types – like orb lightning.

He was now approaching the point of the light's origin when a flash caught his attention, far brighter than anything he'd seen before. It almost looked as though the sky had been cracked open, but surely that was impossible, wasn't it?

Get it together, Eddie. His imagination was getting carried away again.

But there it was a second time, and then a third – as clear as day.

A crack of light, glowing bright-white with the odd hints of blue too, lit the mountainside. It was as if the sky had opened up to swallow the world.

He hurried onwards. He'd now been walking for twenty minutes or so and he'd realised he'd approached the old military base – the place his mom had talked about earlier that day.

Two ominous-looking guard towers stood on either side of the compound, their searchlights beaming out in opposite directions. There was a gated entrance in between them, and a dusty road leading away, which connected the base to the highway. A sparse runway littered with broken pieces of equipment filled the region to the north.

Eddie noted that there was a strange familiarity to this place, but he couldn't quite put his finger on why. As he walked closer, the memories began to surface. He'd often play here, but it had been years since he'd visited. The base was completely abandoned then. The memories of climbing over the gates flooded back. He had no chance of doing that now – it would be impossible, as the gates had been rebuilt almost twice as high, heavily fortified with steel and barbed wire. It was easy to assume that something strange had been happening there.

The lights, Eddie thought. *It all makes sense now. I've discovered a UFO testing ground!*

Eddie had always had an interest in the paranormal. For example, he owned a nice collection of books about the government base located at Groom Lake, Nevada – more commonly known as Area 51. So, to discover a similar base so near to his home was like hitting the jackpot for him. He put in his headphones and turned up the music playing on his smartphone to full-blast.

Excited beyond belief, he decided to investigate further, and hurried along the dusty track towards the compound. He'd taken the cross-country route – through the desert, away from the roads and pathways – and he switched off his flashlight too, to avoid detection by the secret government agents inside.

He reached the fence and edged his way along the perimeter, looking out for any way through. But it had been strengthened, and all of the broken panels were now covered in metal sheeting which had been fixed with industrial strength staples. The people who ran this place clearly didn't want anyone getting inside. Yet, that discovery only made Eddie even more determined to find a way.

A pair of headlights appeared, but Eddie was too busy looking for gaps in the fence to notice. The rev of the vehicle's engine was completely drowned out by the music blasting loudly from his headphones.

He eventually reached the compound's corner, where the fence changed direction.

The glaring lights of the guard towers continued to scan for movement. They were so bright, in fact, that they concealed the headlights of the armoured patrol vehicle which was approaching Eddie from the other side.

The vehicle accelerated.

Eddie walked onwards, completely oblivious to the danger hurtling towards him.

β ⊖

2016-JUL-05 20:35
TURTLEBACK MOUNTAIN,
OUTSIDE TRUTH OR CONSEQUENCES,
NEW MEXICO, UNITED STATES OF AMERICA

Engella awoke from a brief nap to find Annys scanning the compound below. She'd managed to get at least forty minutes' sleep, and she felt a lot better for it.

'I've almost collected everything I need,' said Annys, as she finished reviewing the data on her V-Dis. She pointed towards a settlement of old buildings, which looked as though they were undergoing a series of renovations. The front gates had been fortified and the two guard towers on either side now glared brightly, as their searchlights scanned the surrounding desert.

Engella watched as the V-Dis collected data on everything from air temperature and rock composition through to the background levels of particles

– including neutrinos, photons and the most important one of all: quarks.

'Almost done,' said Annys, tapping her finger on the V-Dis as if doing so would make the device go faster.

Annys could see Engella looking out towards the town and highway they'd noticed earlier that day. 'Truth or Consequences,' Annys said.

'Sorry?' asked Engella, completely confused.

'The town ... It's called Truth or Consequences. Such a fabulous name, don't you think?'

'Yeah, I guess,' Engella replied, as she pondered the unique name.

'That's it, complete,' Annys said, as the V-Dis chimed. 'We have a full scan of the base. All exit points are fully documented, and we have data on the layout of the complex too.'

'Why do we need to know the exit points?' asked Engella, still unclear on the importance of the base below. 'We're not going in, are we?

'The information will help us immensely,' said Annys. 'That's all I can say for now. Let's get a little closer so we can take some photographs of the perimeter, and then we can get out of this horrid place.'

They meandered down the hillside and arrived at the edge of the exclusion zone.

'I've been thinking about our journey here,' said Annys, while they walked. 'It wasn't as easy as it should have been to find the right place and time. I entered the coordinates, but we kept ending up in the wrong timepoint. With all those shifts happening at once, the light show would have been visible for miles.'

'Well let's hope nobody saw it,' Engella said, suddenly rather concerned.

'I have a feeling my shiftband's calibration is way off. We'll need to fix it.'

'I noticed the Hunters were having a much easier time tracking me when I was in New Shanghai,' Engella said. 'Maybe it's the same issue?'

'Yes, dear...sounds like it. Once the calibration is off, it'll be really difficult to pinpoint the coordinates we're aiming for. You'd move around it, without ever really zeroing in on the right space-time coordinates. The worst thing is we'll be leaving behind a trail of quarks that way. We may as well invite the Hunters over for tea and cake.'

'How do we prevent it?' asked Engella.

'Let's just keep it in mind the next time we move,' said Annys. 'We'll need to ensure we limit the number of shifts as much as possible. Also, we should remember that no technology is foolproof. This is new technology after all, so it's inevitable we'd find a few bugs along the way.'

Engella considered the facts. 'What's the worst that could happen?' she asked.

Annys chuckled. 'Well, dear, if we were separated and we tried to meet at the same timepoint again while the calibration is off like I think it is, we could be separated by *years*. Now that would be bad – in fact, it may be impossible to find each other again.'

Engella was worried by this news. 'That is bad,' she said. 'Well. I guess it's good we're sticking together then.'

'It is indeed,' said Annys.

They'd now reached a vantage point with an unobstructed view of the compound. 'This looks like a good place,' Annys said, as she removed a pair of binoculars from her rucksack.

Annys scanned the gates, focussing on the sign hanging above. They had been met with a rather unwelcome message:

PROPERTY OF
THE HUNTINGTON CORPORATION
TRESPASSERS WILL BE PROSECUTED
USE OF WEAPONS AUTHORISED FOR NON-COMPLIANCE

'Friendly bunch, aren't they?' said Annys. 'We're definitely in the right place...We've found them.' She clicked a button on her shiftband and noted the coordinates in space-time. 'I think we have everything we need. I'll just save this to a data file and we're good to go.' She paused, waiting for the device to chime. 'I'm going to encrypt the file, okay? Only you and I will be able to access the shiftband, so we'll need to come up with a password together. Can you think of anything?'

'How about something from *The Wizard of Oz*?' Engella asked.

'Yes,' Annys said. 'I know ...' She whispered a phrase to the shiftband, which bleeped and chimed, an indication that the password had been saved: 'There's no place like home.'

Engella smiled. 'Perfect,' she said.

They started to pack away their equipment and prepared to leave.

Engella glanced back at the compound. 'That place gives me the chills,' she said.

There was nothing obvious about the place which concerned her, but the fact that she knew it belonged to the Hunters gave the place an eerie, cold feeling. She was about to look away when she noticed a light outside the main perimeter. She could see a patrol vehicle trundling around the corner of the fence, its lights glaring across the desert.

But this wasn't the light she had noticed. She saw it again. This time she noticed something odd about the shrubs which were growing beside the fence. They were rustling.

Strange, Engella thought.

She watched the shrubs a while longer. The rustling intensified and leaves fluttered to the floor. 'Someone's by the fence,' she said. 'Look, Annys, down there!'

Annys peered through her binoculars and spotted the boy instantly, as he strolled along, leaving a mist of sand and dust behind him. She watched where he was walking to and then scanned to the other end of the fence.

The patrol vehicle had now turned the corner and was approaching the boy.

By now, the boy had almost reached the end of the fence where the compound joined the main road. He emerged from the treeline, brushed the leaves from his clothes, and stepped out.

The patrol vehicle continued to hurtle down the road. The boy was about to walk out into its path.

'We have to help him,' said Engella.

'There's no time. It's too late,' said Annys. 'And we can't risk being detected.'

'I need the shiftband,' Engella said. 'Now, Annys!'

Annys reluctantly agreed, then snatched it from her own wrist, and clipped it around Engella's.

Engella felt the cold metal against her skin and experienced a sense of ease – she'd missed her own shiftband, after all. She tapped the device, and after accessing their recently acquired data, she locked onto the boy's position.

'Shift,' she yelled, as she dived headfirst into the open wormhole.

Engella materialised in the boy's path and rolled past him, startling him in the process. She grabbed his arm, and pulled him close, then placed her hand over his mouth so he couldn't scream. After she'd dragged him from the roadside kicking and trying to scream, she led him back into the shrubs.

'They're very dangerous people,' Engella whispered. 'We don't want them finding us, okay?'

Eddie, now stunned into silence, nodded in understanding. Once Engella was sure that the boy wasn't going to yell, she removed her hand from his mouth.

'Where did you come from?' Eddie whispered.

Engella shook her head and placed a finger on her lips, gesturing for the boy to remain quiet.

They observed the patrol vehicle as it slowed

nearby. It trundled onwards, the stones crunching under its tyres. A beam of torchlight scanned the fence in a zigzag while Engella and the boy remained perfectly still, not saying a word.

The torchlight flickered off and the patrol vehicle's ignition sounded. The engine revved and rumbled, and the vehicle drove away. They waited in silence until they could hear the vehicle pick up speed, until it eventually hurtled off towards the main gates.

'Close your eyes,' Engella said, as she gripped the boy's arm. 'Shift.'

'Why...? What the...?' Eddie squealed out a profanity as the two of them fell through the portal and tumbled out a few hundred metres away on the hillside. They dropped face-down into the sand with a thump.

'Woah! That was immense!' said Eddie, as he rolled onto his back.

Annys stood over the two teenagers with her hands on her hips and shook her head. Her jacket flopped open, showing off her blaster which was placed neatly in its holster.

'What's your mom going to do?' Eddie asked, his eyes wide. 'Shoot me...? I won't tell anyone about your super powers, I promise!'

'My mom?' Engella said, surprised. 'She's my friend. And no, she's *not* going to shoot you.'

'Oh,' said Eddie. 'You look alike...'

'Now, dear,' Annys said. 'What are we going to do with you? Eh?'

Eddie lifted himself up and dusted off his clothes. 'Do you work for the government? Are you secret agents? Did you cause the lights I've been seeing?' he asked, barely stopping to breathe. 'I want to know everything!'

'Woah, kiddo. Slow down. Let's start with our names first, shall we?' said Engella.

Eddie grinned. 'Yeah, sure,' he said, as he kicked his foot around the sand. 'My name's Eddie.'

'Nice to meet you, Eddie. I'm Engella. And this is Annys.'

Annys smiled, 'Pleased to meet you.'

'Hey,' Eddie said.

'You do know this is restricted property, don't you?' Annys asked.

'Yeah? So, why are you here then?' Eddie said, the sarcasm in his voice shining through.

'Nobody likes a smart-arse, dear,' Annys replied, narrowing her eyes. She relaxed, and her smile returned. 'But seriously, what are you doing here? This place is very dangerous.'

'I'm an investigative journalist,' Eddie said. 'I'm going to write a story about this place and tell the world about all the crazy things that go on here.'

'Oh really,' Engella said, 'and why would anyone believe you?'

'Because I have proof! That's why!' Eddie yelled, as he pulled out his smartphone. He opened up the folder of photographs stored on his phone and showed them to Engella. 'These are photos of aliens. They usually land on the mountain. Somewhere around ... erm, wait a minute. This is the place! Their lights are so bright they illuminate the whole mountainside. That's when their warp systems go into hyperdrive or something!'

'I think you've been watching too many television shows, dear.' Annys said, but it was clear she was now concerned as her eyes met Engella's briefly.

'Look!' Eddie yelled. 'I'll show you!' He snatched back the smartphone and flicked through the images. 'This is the best one,' he said. 'I got this earlier this evening – I was much closer so I was able to zoom in. You can see the aliens coming out of their ship!'

Annys dipped her spectacles so she could see up close, and peered at the screen. The image showed two figures on the hillside, with a bright wormhole shining between them.

'Oh dear,' Annys said. 'We're going to need to have a talk. I think it's best you delete all of your photos so the, erm, government doesn't find them. They'll come looking for you otherwise.'

'Yeah, right!' yelled Eddie. 'You expect me to believe that? You're part of the cover-up! I bet you're here to destroy the evidence!'

'I'm serious,' Annys said. 'You'll need to delete the photographs. Otherwise I'll need to confiscate your phone.'

'You can't do that!'

'I can. And I will,' Annys said, as she placed her hand on her holster.

Eddie looked at the weapon and let out a gulp.

Engella could see that the scare tactics appeared to be working, so she decided to join in – it was for the boy's benefit, after all. 'Now, if you know what's good for you, you'll get out of here and never come back,' she said.

'I live down the road. Why shouldn't I come back? This is my home,' Eddie replied, his voice a little shaky.

'Because it's dangerous, that's why,' Annys said, her face as stern as steel.

Engella sighed. 'Look, you don't want to get involved in any of this, believe me, it's best you get going now. Okay, kiddo?'

'Yes, dear, it's probably better you don't hang around here. It's not safe,' Annys said.

'You know about the lights, don't you?' Eddie asked bluntly. 'You're going to tell the newspapers, and you want the story for yourself.'

Annys looked at Engella, who wasn't pleased at all. 'Eddie, darling, you seem like a clever boy,' she said. 'The people down there in the compound are very dangerous. Promise me you'll leave here and never come back.' She glared at the boy, so he knew she was being serious about the matter.

'Okay, I'll go,' Eddie said. He turned away, when Annys cleared her throat.

'Aren't you forgetting something?' Annys asked, as she held out her hand.

Eddie sighed, and then reached out with his smartphone. He clicked through the folders on his device until the screen read: *delete all*. He clicked it.

'Thank you, Eddie. You did the right thing.'

'What did you do to me earlier? What was that thing we went through? Some kind of tunnel?'

Engella's eyes met with Annys's. She wasn't sure

whether to answer honestly or not, but Annys beat her to it, anyway.

'We can't say anymore, dear. It's too dangerous,' Annys said.

'Okay, I won't ask any more questions. But only if you answer me one thing,' Eddie said.

'I guess it doesn't matter. You did see our new transport system after all,' Annys said, this time glaring at Engella.

'It's a tunnel through space and time,' Engella said.

'No way!' Eddie yelled. 'Cool!'

'Now listen up, kiddo,' Engella said.

'Stop calling me kiddo, will you?! I'm thirteen. I'm not a kid!'

Annys interrupted. 'The less you know the better. This place is going to change. And it's going to change for the worse. We'll be back, but it won't be for a very long time – and you'll be long gone by then. You need to get out of here and carry on like none of this ever happened, okay?'

Eddie nodded, not sure how to respond.

'Where do you live, anyway?' asked Engella.

'I live with my mom, down the road.'

'Promise me, Eddie. Stay away,' Engella said. 'Look after yourself, and look after your mom, too.'

'I promise.'

'It's for the best, Eddie,' Engella said with a warm smile.

'Will I ever see you again?' asked Eddie.

'It's unlikely,' said Annys.

'Okay. Well. If you do ever come back, don't forget to look me up,' Eddie said. 'I live beside Maria's Restaurant and Motel, it's my mom's business. We do the best pancakes in Truth or Consequences.'

'Sounds delightful,' said Annys.

'Now, you'd better get going,' Engella said. 'Bye, kiddo.'

'Bye, Engella.'

They watched Eddie as he traversed down the hillside, away from the compound like they'd agreed. They waited until he was out of sight before they headed back up the hillside towards the mountain.

They didn't have the chance to notice that Eddie had already opened the smartphone's backup memory files. He'd now clicked through to the 'retrieve all' function, and within a few seconds he'd recovered every single photograph.

Eddie was a stubborn boy. He was completely oblivious to the fact that his decision to ignore Annys's wishes would change his life forever.

2016-JUL-05 20:59
COMPOUND, OUTSIDE TRUTH OR CONSEQUENCES, NEW MEXICO, UNITED STATES OF AMERICA

Lera lay on her front and scanned the desert below, her binoculars gripped tightly between her gloved hands. After leaving the Isle of Skye, she'd materialised on the upper slopes of a mountain. She had the perfect vantage point, which gave her a panoramic view of the compound below. The ideal location for a stakeout.

After detecting a surge of quarks, she'd tracked the wormhole activity to the perimeter of the outer fence, next to a road which surrounded the base.

Lera was close, she could feel it. It wouldn't be long before she caught up with the criminals who'd injured Tala, which meant it wouldn't be long until they'd get what was coming to them.

A vehicle sped along a road, its wheels creating a cloud of dust which blew along the track.

'Where are you?' Lera asked, as she continued to scan the region. Her eyes followed the vehicle as it sped towards the compound's gates.

And then she saw them. Three people standing together, halfway up the hillside – a young boy with the two targets.

Lera grinned. 'I've got you,' she said. She moved to her V-Dis, and quickly tapped in a command to activate it. 'Come on, come on!' she yelled.

The device began to whir as it downloaded data on the volume and type of quark, helping to identify the signature of the shiftband. Unbeknown to the targets, every shiftband had its own unique signature.

Once Lera had discovered theirs, she'd be able to track them instantly. No more chasing quarks through space and time. She'd hit them, head on, with everything the Hunters had. 'Any minute now,' she said, as she paced across the rocky plateau.

She examined the graphs, ensuring the quark levels were stable before she continued. She looked back through the binoculars to see that the two targets had now moved away from the other person, who was now walking towards the town. She ignored him and focussed all of her efforts on the targets, who were walking the other way. 'Come on,' she yelled. 'Hurry up!'

The computer buzzed and the screen was filled with numerical values and lights which buzzed and flashed, before a holographic projection of a map in space-time appeared above her. She watched as a small light blinked in red on the map, like a glowing X on a pirate's map. Once the targets shifted again – the blinking light would follow – as it tracked them like a beacon in space-time.

The comm buzzed, and Sykes's voice boomed over the speaker.

'What is it?' Lera snapped. 'I'm busy!'

'Looks like a timeline clean-up is needed, after all. Some photographs made it onto the web. Coordinates say they originated from your current timepoint. The photos will be uploaded tomorrow – in your time – and they'll gain considerable press interest. We'll need to get rid of them ASAP.'

'What photographs?' Lera asked.

'Photos of the targets. One of them shows two figures emerging from a wormhole.'

'Damn it,' Lera said. 'Have you identified the source?'

'Yeah, already done... photos originated from a

smartphone linked to an address not far from you – looks like a restaurant down the highway. Historical records show the place was once owned by a Maria Reyes.'

'I trust you'll be paying Maria a visit then, won't you, boss?' Lera asked.

'Already on my way.'

'Do whatever's necessary. Just make it quick.'

'I'm on it. Sykes out.'

Lera watched as the targets walked along the hillside. They eventually reached a plateau, where they activated their shiftband and left through a portal in a flash of light. She pointed her V-Dis at the wormhole, and scanned it as it faded away. She watched the blinking light on her map shoot across the screen, as the targets rocketed their way to another place and time. 'I've got you,' she said.

Wherever or whenever the targets travelled, Lera would be able to follow. She'd tracked the signature of their shiftband to a fraction of a million units. They could go anywhere, but with her mapping technology, she'd be right behind. They'd soon be caught and Lera would be rewarded handsomely for her work. She'd finally make her mark on the Company – and she'd gain the respect she deserved.

And the best thing of all, Lera had determined, was that the targets had no idea what was about to hit them.

Not until it was too late.

γ ⚲

2016-JUL-06 07:55
MARIA'S RESTAURANT AND MOTEL,
OUTSIDE TRUTH OR CONSEQUENCES,
NEW MEXICO, UNITED STATES OF AMERICA

The following day, Maria entered the restaurant to open up for the day, and found Eddie was already there. He was sitting in one of the booths which lined each side of the restaurant floor. There was a long shiny counter which circled the bar area, with a kitchen hidden behind.

'What are you up to?' Maria said, suspiciously. 'You're never here this early.'

Eddie looked up in surprise. 'Hey, Mom, I couldn't sleep, so I got up to study. I made myself some breakfast too,' he said, as he pushed away a plate of half-eaten pancakes.

The booth's tabletop was completely covered with

textbooks and study guides. Although, Eddie had stopped looking at them long ago, and was more interested in his smartphone now. He had been looking at the photographs he'd taken and eventually found the one of Engella, Annys and the wormhole. He experienced a twang of guilt – he'd promised Annys he was going to delete them, after all.

'What time's your test today?' Maria asked, breaking the silence. 'You'd better get going if you want to make the school bus.'

'Shoot!' Eddie said, as he placed his smartphone on the table. He'd completely lost track of time. He grabbed his backpack and rushed to the door, turning at the last minute.

'Thanks, Mom,' he said. 'Love you.'

'Good luck, honey. You'll do great, I just know it. Love you too.'

Maria watched as her son ran across the carpark towards the bus stop. She looked down at the booth's table and realised he'd left his smartphone behind. She almost went after him, but it was too late. He was already boarding the school bus.

It doesn't matter, she thought, *He won't need it anyway.* She opened the phone's camera app and began to click through the photographs. She was impressed by her son's style – he was fast becoming a talented photographer, and it was all self-taught. If he could manage to take photographs of this standard with a smartphone, imagine what he could do with a proper camera. Maybe she'd buy him one for his next birthday. She clicked through to the next shot, and the image caught her eye. It looked as though two shadows were immersed in a bright light, and it had an art-house feel to it. She wondered if Eddie had modified the image somehow - it almost looked ethereal; ghost-like. On second thoughts, it was familiar after all. The colours reminded her of the lights she'd seen the other night, in the distance around Turtleback Mountain.

'How strange,' she said, as she looked closely at the image. 'Huh.' She placed the smartphone on the counter, picked up Eddie's dirty plate, and turned to enter the kitchen, when the bell of the restaurant door chimed, surprising her. 'I said you'd better get going!' she said, thinking Eddie had returned. She turned around to see a mountain of a man standing in the doorway.

'Oh! I'm so sorry,' she said. 'I thought you were my son. Welcome to Maria's. Can I get you a drink?'

The man just stood there, staring at her blankly. He barely moved, his expression motionless. After a long pause, he approached the counter, and placed his hand on the smartphone.

'Is this yours?' he asked, his voice hoarse and gravel-like.

'Excuse me, sir, can I help you?'

'I said, is this yours?'

'Well, yes,' Maria said, as she grabbed the smartphone from his hand.

'Name?'

'I'm sorry, what do you want?'

'I said, what's your name?'

Maria now felt incredibly uncomfortable, and she began to back away.

'Like I said already... Maria. This is my restaurant.'

The man didn't say another word, and Maria was fully aware that something wasn't right. She tried to get to the kitchen, but it was too late. It all happened so fast, she didn't even have chance to scream.

She fell to the floor and held her chest in pain. The man hadn't used a typical blaster to shoot her, as that would have required a clean-up crew. Blaster technology didn't exist in this time, after all. Instead, he used a simple handgun, a weapon typical to the place and time. That way, the police would assume it was a robbery which had gone wrong; a clear-cut case, which would only require a limited investigation. They'd never find the killer anyway, even if they tried. He'd be long gone, by then.

The man grabbed the smartphone from Maria's weak hand and left silently through the back door.

Maria tried to drag herself towards the telephone but she didn't have the energy to make it. She rested her cheek on the cold tiled floor and noticed it was turning red.

She cried out, realising what it was.

As she closed her eyes for the last time, all she could see was the image of the man's snake tattoo, etched into her mind.

2066-OCT-23 21:40

YIXING FOREST, GREATER NEW SHANGHAI METROPOLIS

The Yixing Forest, situated on the edge of the New Shanghai Metropolis, was bursting with bamboo, trees, rivers, and streams. The trees were on the cusp of change, their lush green leaves turning to a shroud of red. Wind whistled through the branches, releasing a few stray leaves which floated away on the breeze, down to the moist earth below.

The forest lit up momentarily, flashing from red to pink, as the woodland was flooded with light.

Annys and Engella stepped onto the wet leaves which crunched beneath their boots. They looked at the bamboo all around, and the gigantic redwoods which towered above.

'This place is beautiful,' said Engella, as she gazed into the canopy.

'We're not far from Mirror Lake,' said Annys. 'It's a magical place. I've always wanted to go there.'

'Where exactly are we?'

'Turn around and you'll see,' said Annys.

Engella looked up to see lights as they twinkled through the branches. She was overwhelmed by the stunning vista before her. 'New Shanghai,' she said. 'Incredible.' She stepped along a path of stones to reach a better vantage point: an opening in the canopy with a clear view of the city.

'We'll be heading there tomorrow,' said Annys. 'But first, we need to rest.'

'Thank you,' said Engella.

'For what, dear?'

'I didn't think you'd let me come back.'

'I know you well enough by now, Engella. Once you've set your mind on something, there's no going back.'

'I have to do this,' Engella said. 'I need to know what happened to my parents.'

The view of the New Shanghai Metropolis was breathtaking. Three gargantuan domes floated above the old city, all suspended at varying heights like steps leading to a giant's castle.

Engella had never viewed the city from the ground before, she'd always traversed the upper levels and she'd had no idea of the beautiful views she'd been missing. The city had always seemed so frightening. Yet, it felt different when viewed from this place. They watched as thousands of flickering dots zig-zagged between the domes, as transport pods, vehicles and drones all travelled at high speed.

'According to the map, the place we're looking for is in the upper levels of the second dome,' said Annys.

'Yeah, I'd say that's about right. That would be quite near to the place where Papa left me the holocube,' Engella replied.

Annys nodded. 'Well, that sounds like a good place to start.'

'How do you know this is the right time?' Engella asked.

'I, erm ... I just know.'

'The rules?'

'Yes, dear. What I can say is that tomorrow is the day.'

'Okay,' Engella said, nodding in understanding.

They'd already decided upon a plan to retrieve the remaining shiftbands. They'd approach the city early in the morning, and after taking a transport hub from the old city to the lower dome, they'd travel along the streets by foot. They'd ascend through the passages and tunnels until they reached the cross-over point, which joined the lower and middle domes. It would be a long journey, so they'd need to rest.

In the meantime, they now had the opportunity to enjoy the beauty of the Yixing Forest. They wandered through the trees and observed the leaves as they floated about freely, flowing on the winds like surfers who'd caught the perfect wave.

They'd discovered an autumn paradise.

'Do you like it?' Annys asked.

'Yes, it's wonderful,' said Engella.

The forest was a respite when compared to their journey over the last few days, since they'd left the town of Truth or Consequences. After shifting away from Turtleback Mountain, they'd initiated what Engella had termed a 'multi-shift' – a method she'd perfected during her years on the run.

She'd explained the principles to Annys, who was impressed by the idea. It was a simple yet effective avoidance tactic: travel through space-time and visit multiple times and places in the shortest timeframe possible, if the aim was to settle in one place for an extended period. This time, they'd travelled across three continents and through five different time periods. It was a highly successful method of avoiding the

Ɋ β Ⓗ

Hunters for as long as possible, because they'd need additional time to identify and then follow the quark trail. Also, the break would be beneficial for other reasons, as Engella was exhausted, both physically and mentally. The constant chase and the stress of it all had started to take its toll.

At last, time was on their side. The mission to find the shiftbands would be a challenge and they now had days or possibly even weeks to complete their task.

'We should be protected here,' Annys said. 'The view of our camp from the city is pretty much concealed, and no one really comes this way anymore – not now they have the biodomes up there. Why visit a real forest when you can go to an artificial one, right outside your door?'

The air was damp and the smell of the forest sweet. Rain dripped from the trees, a constant *tip-tap* which echoed all around. Engella closed her eyes and felt the rain on her face. 'I'm going for a walk,' she said. 'It's so beautiful here.'

Annys nodded. 'Okay, dear. Don't be long, okay?'

Engella acknowledged this with a simple nod, before something caught her eye. She stood motionless, her eyes transfixed, drawn to the sounds from within the trees.

'What is it?' Annys asked. She walked over and joined Engella, who was gazing into the forest.

'The leaves, the bamboo...' Engella said. 'The colours – they're so beautiful.'

Annys smiled. 'They are, aren't they?' She placed her hand around Engella's waist.

'I'm always running,' Engella said. 'It's nice to just, you know, enjoy silence sometimes.'

'I know what you mean, dear. This place is wonderful. So very peaceful... That's why I chose it.'

Bird song erupted from a tree beside them. They stood together in silence and enjoyed the spectacle together.

'I won't be long,' Engella said, as she strolled into the undergrowth. The forest exploded with sound. The rain tip-tapped and the wind blew in gusts, while the birds chirped from above. She'd reached a trail through the trees and she paused, listening intently. It wasn't just the rain she could hear. There was a rush of water too, from a nearby stream or river. She followed the sound, edging through the trees, until the rush developed into a roar.

Soon, Engella noticed she had travelled uphill, as the elevation increased slightly. She quickened her pace and approached the raging water in the distance.

The slope became more prominent, with trees growing from the hillside, their exposed roots tangled around each other. Some trees had fallen over completely, while others grew around their fallen comrades as they reached for the light in the canopy above.

Engella eventually saw flashes of white between the trees, and she pushed her way through the final layer of foliage. She burst through into a clearing and discovered she had arrived on the edge of a small cliff. She gasped at the beauty of the raging waterfall beside her, as the deluge of water poured down, heavy with rainwater from the night before. The streams below had merged into violent rapids, and the winds stirred.

Engella could feel spray on her skin, her body cooled by droplets in the air. She closed her eyes and listened to the roar. She took it all in for a moment, and let out a big sigh. She'd not felt this at ease with the world for as long as she could remember. It felt good.

As she gazed into the canopy, the cityscape felt more pronounced. She found the juxtaposition of the city and forest together fascinating: both nature and technology, two opposites, intertwined within the city of New Shanghai.

A gust of wind knocked a flurry of leaves into the air. They floated all around like orange, red, and brown snowflakes. She watched as they fell away into the abyss below.

An hour passed, and Engella returned to where she'd left Annys to find she'd already set up camp. The cube-tent had been activated and was already surrounded by bamboo – an additional level of protection. Engella could see the perimeter sensors placed around the camp evenly, with the closest nestled between two branches of bamboo beside them.

'I found this incredible waterfall,' Engella said, unable to hold back her joy.

'Oh, how wonderful, dear,' said Annys. 'Where did you find it?'

Engella explained the route she had taken, and Annys was intrigued. 'Let's go for a walk later and you can show me,' she said.

'Oh yes, I'd love that,' Engella said.

'So, dinner tonight is sushi, then. It's all we have left. But I have a feeling we'll be able to restock on our mission tomorrow.'

Annys pulled out the remaining food tablet with a picture of a sushi roll on top. She'd already prepared the Tri-Key, and after she poured some water over it and heated the freeze-dried food it burst outwards into a giant California roll; more than enough for two.

'What time do we head off tomorrow?' Engella asked.

'Let's get up early,' Annys replied. 'We can take a nice stroll to the old city and find the transport hub. That way we can pick up some supplies along the way.'

'I've always wondered about the old city,' Engella said.

'Yes, they built the new one above it. Fascinating, really. Besides, I don't think we should be leaving this wonderful place anytime soon. I'd say we should stay here a few days at least. Don't you think?'

Engella smiled.

'We'll find a place to stay in the middle dome. Somewhere with a roof this time.'

'Sounds good to me.'

They ate their meal and considered the task before them. It wasn't going to be easy. The city was full of spies, their eyes and ears always ready to feed information into the Hunters' network. Their refuge wouldn't stay safe for long. Still, they had to carry on. It was vital they completed their mission, whatever the cost.

The night was cold. The droplets which coated the branches of the bamboo forest had already hardened to ice, and the breeze was harsh and bitter.

Inside the tent, Annys was already fast asleep but Engella was too chilly to get comfortable. The temperature had dropped considerably, and she could see her breath. She burrowed deeper into her sleeping bag and zipped it tightly over her head.

A high-pitched whistle from deep within the forest startled her. Annys stirred momentarily, turning over, before settling again. Engella didn't move a muscle, listening intently, and tried to make out the noise again. But there was nothing. The forest was silent. She relaxed a little. It was probably just an owl or some other nocturnal creature. Though, it didn't sound like anything she was familiar with.

She was overwhelmed by a wave of nausea, and her head began to throb. Her breathing slowed and she lay motionless as the dread began to build. The prickling feeling on the back of her neck returned and a feeling of terror crept over her.

Suddenly there was a loud crack, but this time closer; so loud that the birds in the trees around them fluttered from their perches. Twigs cracked and branches broke under the weight of whatever was approaching.

They were outside. Engella rolled onto her side and

⚘ β Ⓗ

removed herself from her sleeping bag in one efficient turn. She placed her hand on Annys's shoulder and shook her gently, waking her. Annys looked into Engella's eyes, wide with fear, and knew instantly what was happening.

'We have company,' Engella whispered.

Annys crawled out from her sleeping bag, and grabbed whatever she could find, making sure to pack the essential equipment, while Engella moved to the entrance, ready to unzip the door.

Annys reviewed the V-Dis, about to check the sensor data, but there was nothing – the screen was blank. She tried everything she could to activate it, but it wouldn't work.

'It's dead,' said Annys, 'power's gone... We'd better go. We'll pick up new supplies somewhere else. Let's get out of here.'

Engella agreed and held Annys's hand.

'Shift,' said Annys, ready to step through the portal, but there was nothing. The shiftband wasn't working, either. Something was terribly wrong.

'My head...' Engella said, as she grabbed her temples.

'You're feeling the effects of the wormholes again,' Annys said. 'They're coming for us.' She unzipped the top half of the tent door slowly and scanned the canopy.

And there it was.

The drone hovered silently, its single glaring eye staring at them like a glistening ruby.

Annys gestured towards it. 'Blocker-drone. It's jamming everything,' she said. 'They've drained all of our power... means the sensors will be down too.'

With their equipment jammed, their tent was no longer invisible. Their camouflage was gone.

Engella reached for the blaster, her hands trembling, and pointed it towards the entrance.

Annys placed her hand on Engella's shoulder. 'It's okay,' she said, 'We can do this.'

A long shadow appeared across the side of the tent lit by moonlight, as the intruder crept towards them.

'We need to make a run for it,' Engella said. She gestured with her hand as she instructed Annys which way to go.

The silence of the forest had been replaced by noise; they were no longer alone. They could hear voices in the distance; shouts, whistles and laughter. The voices mocking their victims as they approached.

'Remember our plan, okay?' said Annys. 'We've prepared for this. Just remember everything we discussed. Follow the plan, and we'll be okay.'

'I'll remember.'

'Now,' said Annys. With that, Engella directed an energy bolt through the side of the tent, blasting most of it away in the process.

The Hunter groaned as he slumped forwards into what remained of the tent. The explosion was deafening and echoed through the trees.

Engella grabbed Annys's hand and pulled her into the night. They smashed their way through the branches in their path, pulling their way through the tangled undergrowth, which ripped at their exposed skin like tiny knives.

They slid across a mass of leaves and splashed through mud.

Annys began to lag behind, unable to keep the pace, her breathing fast. Engella pulled back and returned to help her friend climb across a log which had collapsed in their path.

'I can't, dear, I can't anymore,' Annys said, unable to catch her breath.

'Yes, you can!' Engella yelled, pulling at her arm. 'This way,' she said, as she pointed to the hillside.

They screamed out as shock-grenades exploded all around, the tress burning as the force knocked them backwards into the undergrowth.

The drone was above them now, following their

every move like a hawk above its prey. Engella pointed the blaster, fired, and the drone exploded, sending metal and plastic pieces raining down.

Annys ran over to the smoking remains and picked through them, eventually removing a tiny emitter – an inhibitor, its blue eye still bright. She deactivated it and watched as the blinking eye faded to black.

'Take this,' said Annys, as she placed the emitter in Engella's hand. 'Turn it on as soon as you're safe. It's incredibly important.'

Engella understood and placed the inhibitor in her pocket.

The forest lit up, and space-time warped.

The Hunters' portals emerged all around – they were under attack by a squad, and they were surrounded. They held each other, not sure which way to go.

Annys tapped a code into her shiftband, and the system beeped and buzzed a confirmation in reply. She was about to issue the command to shift, when a Hunter materialised beside them. The Hunter grabbed her arm, but she managed to pull away. She ripped the shiftband from her wrist and snapped it over Engella's.

'We need to separate,' Annys yelled. 'It's our only

hope. Go to the place you found, you know, the place you wanted to show me ... I'll meet you there.'

Engella shook her head. 'I won't leave you,' she said, as her eyes welled up.

'The coordinates are set, you just need to shift!' Annys sobbed, unable to let go of Engella's hand. The Hunter grabbed for the both of them this time, but Annys blocked him from Engella.

'Go!' Annys said, as she pushed Engella forwards, the force so strong she almost knocked her to the ground. Annys managed to pull away from the Hunter, but he was close behind, grabbing at Annys with his skeletal fingers.

Engella turned and ran into the forest, traversing over twigs and branches, and finding it difficult to keep her footing in the blackness of night. She remembered the route, as she'd memorised it from her walk, but it was more difficult in the dark. She could hear the shouts of Hunters as they poured from the portals in droves.

She'd never experienced an attack of this magnitude.

Engella sprinted, her only chance left was to reach the waterfall in time to meet Annys. She stumbled over a tree stump, grazing her leg on a sharp protruding branch. She wanted to yell out, but instead all she could do was wince and fight through the pain. If she made the slightest noise, the Hunters would certainly find her.

Q   Q   Q

The Hunters marched into the forest, cloaked in black, their blasters aimed and ready to fire. The squad edged forwards; a group of four in the centre carrying standard weapons, while two were placed on either side each holding flamethrowers. They sent little bursts of fire into the air to light the way ahead, but some of the flames set the canopy alight.

Sykes stood with his hands on his hips watching from afar, chewing gum noisily.

'Is that really necessary?' Lera asked, as she gestured towards the flames. 'Surely we can use standard lighting?'

'Nothing like a good scare, cadet,' Sykes said, grinning. Lera could see his gold teeth glinting in the light from the flames.

Lera shook her head. 'We should probably keep the damage to a minimum,' she said, as she watched burning branches collapse to the ground.

'You know me, Lera, I like to cause a scene. And anyway, the clean-up crew will sort it all out afterwards. We may as well have a little fun, along the way. Don't you think?'

Lera wasn't sure why the capture of two criminals required such theatre, yet she was unwilling to challenge her commanding officer. She nodded and headed towards the forest. The bushes rustled up ahead, and it wasn't long before she'd spotted Engella as she ran through the trees up the hillside. An older woman hobbled into the undergrowth unsteady on her feet, going the opposite way.

'Now we know who was helping her,' Lera said as she pointed towards the woman.

'We're on,' Sykes said, as he prepared his weapon. He gestured towards the woman. 'You take her. Engella's mine.'

๑   ๑   ๑

Engella scrambled through the undergrowth, trying not to slip as the rain began to pour. A shock-grenade exploded, the sonic boom blasting so loud her ears rang. She held her head to catch her breath and, as fast as she could, pulled herself over stumps and rocks which littered the mud-filled trail.

Sykes was suddenly in Engella's path, his weapon locked and loaded. He pulled the trigger and sent a glowing ball of fire hurtling forwards. Engella dived into the undergrowth as it exploded with a ferocious boom. She placed her hands over her ears and lay in the dirt. She wanted so very much to yell out, but bit her tongue and held it in. A log had fallen on its side, its branches crunched and cracked from the force of the shock-grenade's explosion. She dragged herself towards the log, scraping her fingers through the mud, finally taking shelter beneath.

'Come out, come out wherever you are,' Sykes said, laughing as he spoke. 'Itsy bitsy spider, climbed up the water spout... Down came the rain and washed the spider out.'

Engella shivered at the Hunter's sick taunts. She'd come across some awful people in her time, but this man was particularly nasty. It was as if he really got a kick out of hurting people.

Sykes's boots crunched the leaves and twigs on the bank above Engella's head. She tried to remain silent and held her breath; too scared to move in case he heard her.

She heard a crack and a loud groan, then Sykes dropped motionless over the log like a broken rag-doll and she watched as he tumbled down the hillside. She tried to work out where he'd been hit from, but there was nothing there. After pulling herself to her feet, she checked the path ahead.

Torchlight flashed through the trees, but it was going the other way.

She finally had her chance to make a run for the waterfall. She was so close, so she fought through the pain and exhaustion until she reached the summit. She entered the clearing – before a place of such beauty. Now, full of sadness and fear. She stopped running, completely out of breath.

Annys was there waiting for her, just as she'd promised. But she was shaking, with her hands held out, tied in yellow cable.

Engella looked into her friend's eyes. She'd never seen her this way: broken, her eyes full of terror.

Two Hunters held her arms, their blasters pointed at her back.

'Are you going to come quietly?' Tala snapped, as she emerged from the shadows of the trees.

Engella's heart rate raced. She froze with fear, as the terror of the cottage came crashing back; hitting her like a freight train. She stayed silent, watching as the Hunter paced along the plateau.

'Answer me!' Tala said, narrowing her eyes. 'You thought I was dead, didn't you?'

Lera Tox appeared next, running from the hillside. 'Sykes is hurt, Commander,' she said. 'It was the criminals, they injured him. Looks pretty serious too.'

'Another crime for the list!' Tala said, as she pulled out a knife from her belt. She edged closer to Annys and dragged the blade along her arm, leaving behind a trail of red and making Annys wince in pain.

'Don't hurt her!' Engella yelled.

'Oh, you do have a voice, after all. You just injured one of my men. How about I do the same to this one?'

'I didn't do anything!' Engella shouted, as tears streamed down her face.

'You're full of lies, Engella,' Tala snapped. 'Put your weapon down. Otherwise she dies.'

The Hunters who had secured Annys pushed their blasters deeper into her back, yet she remained defiant, pushing back at them, using the little amount of energy she had left.

Engella looked around, trying to formulate a plan.

'Don't even bother,' Tala said.

Think. There must be a way out of this, Engella thought. Although, she knew it was futile. There was only one thing she could do now. She looked Annys in the eyes. There was no way she could break her free, there were just too many of them. Engella knew what she had to do.

Annys mouthed one word: 'Go.'

As she raised her wrist, Engella whispered to the shiftband: 'There's no place like home.'

Engella's gaze didn't leave Annys's for a second, not until her vision blurred.

'No!' Tala yelled, as she rushed forwards, grabbing at Engella.

The remaining Hunters turned their weapons towards the swirling vortex, but they were too late. Engella was already immersed in a whirlpool of light.

She cried out, as she fell into the void.

γ �

2016-JUL-06 10:04

HOT SPRINGS HIGH SCHOOL,
TRUTH OR CONSEQUENCES,
NEW MEXICO, UNITED STATES OF AMERICA

Eddie's test was already underway, and he'd managed to answer the first question with relative ease. The extra study he'd completed that morning had been a good decision after all. His teacher, Mr Anderson, sat at the front of the room. He'd be pleased with Eddie's progress and the additional work he had put in. Eddie could feel it.

The room was quiet, as the students worked hard to get through the questions in the available time. They were sat in four rows, with each table set up in a similar manner. They included a test paper, a pencil and sharpener to work, and an eraser for any mistakes they happened to make.

The sun was bright, and light shone through the large glass windows on the side. The tables had been placed closer to the wall and away from the windows, so that the students wouldn't be uncomfortable in the heat.

Eddie was about to begin the algebra question, when there was a loud knock at the classroom door. It opened just enough for the principal to step in, who then proceeded to summon Eddie's teacher to the door. The interruption frustrated Eddie, as it made him lose his train of thought. He glanced back at his test paper, and tried to focus again, but all he could hear were voices chattering, now that the children had been disturbed. He tried to see what all the commotion was about, but he was sat in the middle of the room, so he couldn't see who was outside.

Mr Anderson returned, and paced beside the door, his face sombre. 'Eddie,' he said. 'Can you come with me, please?'

Eddie was startled to be called out by name. What had he done? And why would they take him out of class during a test? 'Uh, okay?' he said, confused. He went to the door, without saying a word. He stepped into the corridor to see the sheriff standing there, her hands gripped tightly.

Mr Anderson placed his hand on Eddie's shoulder. 'You'll need to go with the sheriff, okay?' he said softly.

'What's wrong?' Eddie asked, but Mr Anderson didn't reply.

'Hello, Eddie,' the sheriff said. She held open the door of an empty classroom further down the corridor and gestured for him to go inside. She followed him in and closed the door behind them.

The principal remained in the corridor, but paced nervously. She observed through the glass of the classroom door, as the sheriff began to speak.

She looked down in sorrow when the boy cried out – a horrendous wail, as his world came crashing down around him.

β ⚷

1954-MAR-17 02:17
RUBHA SHLÈITE, SKYE, SCOTLAND

The portal flashed wide open with an explosion of sparks. Engella tumbled out and landed with a thud in the dirt. It was the dead of night, and a storm was brewing: gale-force winds made it difficult to stand still, while a deluge of rain made it impossible to see. She squinted and covered her eyes from the rain and tried to make out where she was. A flash of lightning helped her along, the light so bright that the beach and ocean suddenly appeared beside her. Waves as big as houses crashed against the rocks below. She had arrived by the edge of a cliff, and the surprise of seeing the drop disorientated her, so she spun around and stumbled forwards, almost losing her balance in the process.

She shivered in the freezing wind and began to sob. She cried out in anger at her situation and fell to her knees. She hadn't felt a loss of this magnitude since she was a little girl.

It was like the day she had lost her parents, all over again. But this time, instead of imagining her mother's face, all she could see was Annys held at gunpoint, her eyes wide with fear. Anxiety overwhelmed the girl. She was heartbroken, and she'd finally reached the limit of what she was able to cope with. The Hunters had utterly broken her this time, and she didn't know what to do.

How could I have left her? she thought, as she replayed the events at the waterfall repeatedly. She experienced an overwhelming feeling of guilt. All she wanted to do now was to curl up and forget all about it. Yet she knew that she needed to compose herself and push forward, however difficult it would be.

Engella remembered how Annys had rummaged through the remains of the drone. She reached into her pocket and pulled out the device which Annys had passed to her before they were attacked. She wasn't sure how it worked but she activated it anyway, as Annys had instructed her to. A blue light on the base of the device began to blink.

Another flash of lightning illuminated the beach again. Engella could make out the rocks and stones, which lined the pathway that led away from the beach. She'd found her bearings and she'd worked out where she was, as her eyes finally adjusted to the dark.

There's no place like home.

They'd agreed to use their secret password in the event they were separated, and Engella now understood why. Annys had mentioned that she'd already programmed the shiftband with coordinates.

She'd sent her back to the Isle of Skye.

Although, on checking the shiftband, Engella realised she'd shifted many years into the past, a long time before the events at Annys's cottage. The place made sense – it was Annys's home after all.

But why had she sent her to this time? It didn't quite add up, so she decided she'd go back to the cottage. Perhaps she'd learn more there, and it would also give her time to decide upon her next moves.

She hurried through the forest in the pouring rain and followed the route which Annys had shown her, until eventually she found the clearing.

Instead of approaching the cottage, she planned her escape route, in case the need arose. She had to be prepared for anything, in case the Hunters showed up. Once she had decided it was safe, Engella moved closer. The lights were off, and it didn't look as though anyone was at home, but it was the middle of the night after all.

She tried the doorknob, but the cottage was locked, as she'd expected. It was time to use a trick she'd learned on the streets, and she removed a needle from her utility belt, placing it inside the locking mechanism.

The lock clicked and the door jolted, until Engella was able to release the catch. She listened for any movement inside and was concerned momentarily when she thought she'd heard a shuffle from the floor above. This time she listened intently, but the cottage was silent except for the patter of the rain hitting the roof.

Suddenly, the stairs and landing were flooded with light, and a male voice shouted from the room above. 'Who's there?!' he asked.

Alarmed, Engella stepped backwards, and bumped into the door which clattered open.

She didn't even need to think – she had to get out of there – and bolted out of the door, not looking back until she'd made it into the trees.

Once she had concealed herself amidst the undergrowth, she watched while the rest of the cottage lit up. It looked as though the person inside had switched on every single light in the entire cottage.

Engella waited patiently and after some time, the lights of the cottage began to go out. She hoped the man had assumed by this point that the door had been blown open by the gale, and glossed over the fact that gales were not usually that successful at unlocking locked doors.

Engella decided to go further into the woods, as she felt too exposed. She came across a small wood-panelled structure a few minutes' walk away, and was pleased to find that the door was unlocked. Inside, small logs were stacked neatly in rows along the walls, while gardening tools and utensils were placed on small hooks hanging from the ceiling. They could easily be used for protection if the need arose. Engella decided it was a good place to rest for the night. She didn't have the luxury of a cube-tent, after all.

What I wouldn't give to sleep in the cottage right now. Still, she reminded herself that she'd dealt with worse sleeping arrangements than these. The low levs of New Shanghai were first to come to mind. The woodstore was by no means perfect, but she'd make the best of it.

Engella had so many questions. Who was the man in the cottage? And why had Annys sent her here?

She needed to know more about him. His behaviour hadn't been very Hunter-like. Hunters didn't call out ahead, they stalked their prey and pounced at the last second. He actually seemed frightened, as if he thought she was the intruder. Yet, she told herself that she shouldn't make any assumptions, just in case it was a ploy to catch her off guard. She would investigate further, and perhaps – if all was well – she'd even drum up the courage to approach him in person. But she'd wait until she could be certain that she would be safe. She settled into the woodstore for the night, and eventually managed to fall sleep.

She was awoken the next morning by the sound of geese flying overhead, and a very loud wood pigeon cooing in the tree outside. Sunlight began to shine through the gaps in between the wood panelling, and Engella decided it was the right time to get up. Considering the noisy wake-up call she'd received, she was surprised overall at how well she'd slept. In fact, the woodstore had turned out to be warmer than she'd expected. She pulled her hair back into a ponytail and tied it loosely, before putting on her large black boots. She went outside to find the storm had cleared: the sky was blue, and there was only the occasional wisp of cloud. The weather ahead looked as though it would be more to her liking.

Quietly, Engella returned to the woods beside the cottage, and explored the treeline until she found a vantage point with a direct line of sight into the kitchen window.

She waited, and observed carefully, but the cottage was silent. She checked the time and noted that it was just after six o'clock in the morning. It was still early, so she decided she'd wait for a while longer before attempting to investigate further. Her mind began to wander, and she found herself thinking about Annys. Where was she now? And more importantly, was she even alive?

She felt a twinge of anxiety when she noticed someone stirring inside, and she was startled by the sudden appearance of a man at the back door. He had pale white skin and he was tall – quite lanky in fact – and his black hair was greased back neatly all the way. He wore tortoise-shell horn-rimmed glasses and he was only half-dressed, his white undervest not equalling the standard of his smart pinstriped suit trousers or shiny shoes. He spent a few moments enjoying the hanging baskets of flowers on each side of the door, and eventually sat down on a bench in front of the petunias. He reached into his pocket and lit his pipe, then puffed out a little cloud of smoke from his nose and mouth.

He scanned the treeline and when looking in her direction, he narrowed his eyes.

Engella didn't move a muscle. She was certain she'd been seen but his stare soon moved elsewhere. If he'd seen her, he definitely hadn't made it obvious.

Who are you? And why are you inside Annys's cottage? The man looked friendly enough. He had a kind face, the kind of face a doctor or teacher would have.

The man eventually finished his pipe and went back inside. After the door had slammed shut, Engella relocated herself so she had a better view through the window. She watched the man as he sat in his armchair and flicked through the pages of a newspaper.

Engella hadn't seen a newspaper in years. All modes of communication in the 2060s were high-tech – via computer node, V-Dis, or hologram, except for her journal of course.

The man left the cottage at eight o'clock on the dot. Engella edged closer, waiting until she was sure the man had gone outside before she made her way to the outside wall. She peered around and watched as he climbed inside his sky-blue BMW 501. Her eyes were drawn to the vehicle's metallic wheel trims, which were reflecting the morning sun.

The man checked his mirrors and proceeded to reverse down the drive. After a six-point turn, which he was obviously unhappy about – based on the number of times Engella had seen him mumble to himself, he finally drove off down the road.

Engella waited until the car's engine was only a tiny buzz in the distance, and proceeded to unlock the door.

Thankfully, once inside, there didn't appear to be any technology in sight, and there was nothing to suggest that the man was a Hunter in disguise. Although, Engella pondered, that would be exactly what a secretly disguised Hunter would want her to think. She'd remain alert, and she'd continue to look for evidence upstairs. However, as she was about to go she felt a pang of hunger and her stomach rumbled loudly, drawing her focus to the kitchen. It made her realise that she hadn't eaten for nearly a whole day, so she immediately made her way to the pantry.

The shelves were stocked to the brim, and after several minutes of indecision, Engella decided upon toast for breakfast and removed a loaf of bread from the bottom shelf. After exploring inside the refrigerator, she discovered the butter tray as well as a little jar of marmalade.

Don't mind if I do, Engella thought, after she'd buttered a slice of bread and smothered it with a dollop of orangey goodness.

Once she was full up with breakfast, she decided it was time to look around. She was very aware that she didn't yet know the man's schedule so she remained alert, and kept an eye out for the car, by making regular checks of the road which led away from the cottage.

First of all, Engella approached the man's bedroom and peered around the door. The room was neat and tidy, with everything in its place. She opened the wardrobe to find several pinstripe suits and a number of white shirts all hanging neatly, while an assortment of ties and shoes were all laid out on shelves. Whoever this man was, it was obvious he took pride in his appearance.

Next, Engella moved to a chest of drawers in the corner of the room. A lamp sat on top, placed to one side, while a gold-framed photograph sat in the middle. There was a black and white photograph inside, of the man holding a young baby. Engella was quick to note that the photograph was taken outside the cottage, as she recognised the ivy that surrounded the door.

She explored the chest, reviewing the contents of the drawers one by one, until eventually she reached the bottom. Inside, there were envelopes addressed to the man, written by hand in blue ink. Engella admired the lettering. She found it quite beautiful. There was something to be said about the days before technology, when keyboards and voice-activated writing bots were yet to be invented. The simplicity of life was appealing.

It was quite unusual for people to write by hand in Engella's time, which was exactly the reason why Engella continued to write by hand in her journal. It reminded her of her mother who'd often write by hand in her own diary. It felt more personal that way, so she'd decided at an early age to follow the tradition herself. It felt rawer to write by hand and allowed her to express herself with greater clarity. Whenever she felt sad or frightened, she'd write a journal entry and was able to cope a little better. Sometimes, she'd read over the entry until she knew the words off by heart. That way she owned the experience and was able to take a little power away from the Hunters.

Engella picked up one of the letters and noticed they had all been addressed to the same person.

Dr Patrick Munro
Elgol Cottage
Claigan
Isle of Skye
Scotland

'Patrick Munro,' she said. 'At least I know your name now.' She placed the letters back where she'd found them, closed the drawers, and returned to the photograph placed on the top. She examined it closely. Patrick was wearing another pinstripe suit and the baby was dressed in a white gown.

The child was holding a toy – small, reflective and cube-shaped. At first, Engella thought it looked like her holocube, but she knew that was impossible. Nonetheless, there was something unusual about the image but Engella couldn't quite put her finger on what it was.

Engella looked around one last time, to make sure everything had been returned to its place. She moved to the hallway and opened up the cupboards. The shelves inside were well organised, with piles of bedsheets and blankets folded in stacks, but there was nothing of real interest – until she noticed something pushed towards the back of the top shelf.

She reached up and discovered it was a carefully packed wooden box, painted red with black ladybird spots. She managed to retrieve it without spilling the contents and she opened the lid, surprised to find it was full of toys. They were the old-style type of toy, simple in their design and build. There wasn't a single Friendly-bot or artificially-intelligent teddy bear in sight. She wondered how people ever managed to live without technology. Everything must have been so much more difficult. She picked up a rag doll wearing a blue checked dress and it reminded her of Dorothy from *The Wizard of Oz*. She looked over a small wooden horse and ran her fingers through the fur of a stuffed rabbit.

Why does the man have a box of toys? she asked herself, and decided it was time to explore further. As she entered the second bedroom, the place where she'd spent the night during her first visit to the cottage, she was completely dazzled by what she saw. The walls of the bedroom were decorated in a beautiful mural of rainbows, fairies and flowers.

It was now crystal clear why Patrick had the box of toys: a child lived there too.

Engella was even more puzzled by this discovery. Why had Annys sent her back to this time? There was no evidence that Annys had ever been there, but she must have had a reason.

Engella pondered her situation. She was now many years in the past, with no plan of where she'd shift to next. She was fully aware that she'd need to limit the number of times she could shift, as the Hunters would be able to track her again. On consideration, why hadn't the Hunters followed her to this place and time? They had clearly found a way to track her shiftband, yet they hadn't followed. Annys must have done something to mask Engella's journey there, otherwise she'd have been in custody by now. She reached inside her pocket and pulled out the small device with the blinking eye, which Annys had removed from the drone. The device inhibited their own shiftband from working, so perhaps it had the same effect on the Hunters' devices too.

Engella returned to the landing when a noise from downstairs caught her attention. She crept to the window and peered outside, relieved to see Patrick's parking space still empty. She'd been inside for several minutes now, so it was probably a good time to make her move. The longer she remained inside, the more likely it was that she'd be discovered.

She hurried downstairs and decided it wouldn't hurt if she took a little more food to eat at lunchtime. She didn't have any other options, after all.

As she entered the kitchen, the lights flashed on.

'I wondered if you'd try to get in again today,' Patrick said. He sat in his armchair, with a pistol in his hand. 'You're not very good at covering your tracks, are you? I parked my car down the road, so you'd think I was out,' he said bluntly, his stare as cold as ice. 'Come closer, let me take a good look at the thief who's been breaking in and stealing my food.'

Engella's heart had almost jumped out of her chest by this point. She was speechless and had almost turned to run, but she already realised it was pointless to try. Instead, she gulped and accepted her fate, and stepped out into the sitting room, so the man could see her properly.

He glared at the girl, his face red, as the anger bubbled upwards. 'How dare you come into my property...' he said, as he looked Engella in the eyes. But all of a sudden, his expression changed. At first his eyes were wide with surprise, and then he almost looked sad. He placed the pistol on the tabletop, as his hands began to tremble.

'M ... May?' he asked.

Engella shook her head, 'No. But how do you know May?' she said.

'May is an old friend of mine,' Patrick said. 'We used to work together.'

At this point, Engella rushed forwards, eager to learn more. Annys *had* sent her there for a reason. Engella was right not to doubt her.

'You know my mother?' Engella asked, her eyes wide.

'Your mother? Who are you?' Patrick asked.

'Engella.'

The man jumped from his chair, ran forwards and placed his hands on Engella's shoulders. 'It can't be! It really can't!' Patrick said, his face full of joy. 'How is this possible?'

Is this really happening?

'Sit down, sit down,' Patrick said, as he gestured for Engella to place herself beside him. 'I'm Dr Patrick Munro. It's so wonderful to see you again.'

'You knew my mother?' Engella asked. 'Have you seen her?'

Patrick's face changed to sadness. 'No. I'm afraid not,' he said. 'Not for a very long time.'

Engella was disappointed by this news, and she wasn't sure what to say next, yet she still had so many questions. Whoever this person was, he'd known her mother. Perhaps even both of her parents. This was the closest she'd been to them for as long as she could remember.

Patrick looked Engella up and down, and he was clearly in shock about something. 'The last time I saw you, you were just a baby,' he said.

Engella pondered this for a moment. 'I haven't seen my parents for eight years,' she said.

'May I ask? Exactly how old *are* you?' Patrick asked.

'I'm seventeen,' said Engella.

'I just don't understand it...' Patrick said. 'Seventeen? How is this even possible?' He placed his hand on the back of a chair to steady himself, while his face had turned from pink to white. He didn't look well at all. Engella didn't really know how to respond to the question. She was seventeen just because she was. The man wasn't making any sense.

'Engella, why don't you come and sit down?' Patrick said. 'We have lots to talk about. I need to ask you some questions.'

Engella edged closer to the sofa, not taking her eyes of Patrick for a second.

'It's okay,' Patrick said. 'I won't bite.' Engella smiled and sat down beside him, waiting for him to speak.

'Where do we even begin?' Patrick asked. 'I don't quite know where to start.'

'I don't either,' Engella said. 'You said you worked with my parents... How about we start there? If that's true, what are you doing in this time period? I checked the data, and if my calculations are correct, we're sometime in the mid-twentieth century.'

'This is 1954,' Patrick replied. 'You don't belong in this time, and neither do I ... but it's my home now.'

Engella was surprised to discover that Patrick was from the future too. She relaxed, as she suddenly felt more comfortable. 'How long have you been here?' she asked. 'In this time period, I mean.'

'To be honest, I stopped counting long ago. But I can probably work it out. It's at least four years ... almost five now.'

'Five years?' Engella asked, quite stunned by this information. 'Is that when you last saw my parents?'

'Yes, that's right. It's been a long time.' Patrick said. He looked Engella directly in the eyes. 'Has anyone ever told you that you're a spitting image of your mother?'

'I am?'

'Yes. I can't quite believe the resemblance ... it's remarkable.'

Engella smiled. 'No, no one's ever told me that,' she

said. A warm feeling welled up inside her. She was proud to discover that she looked like her mother. It made her feel closer to her.

'The last time I saw your parents was in the city of New Shanghai. Have you heard of that place?'

'Yes, I have,' Engella said. 'In fact, I lived there for a while.'

'Ah, I see,' Patrick said. 'We had a research laboratory in the upper levels of the city. We worked there together for a number of years, until...'

'The takeover,' Engella said.

'Well, yes. Once the Company had decided they wanted rid of us, our only option was to make a run for it. My family was from Skye, you see, so we decided upon this place as a meeting point. It's the perfect hideout, no people or buildings for miles. In this time, there is no technology as we know it, so we didn't have to worry about getting tracked by other means – you know, by leaving any type of electronic signature: bank details, social media, et cetera. The problem was, we didn't make it in time. We were meant to come here together, all of us, but we were attacked and became separated. It all happened so quickly.'

'The laboratory you mentioned. Can you give me more information on it?'

'Of course. It was our research lab, at our company: Graviton Dynamics, our old business. It's the place where we developed our technology together ... your parents and I.'

'The shiftbands,' said Engella. She remembered something Annys had told her on the hillside at Turtleback Mountain. Patrick was the other scientist who founded the business with her parents. She pulled out the holocube from her rucksack and tried to activate it, but nothing happened.

'I need to show you something,' Engella said. 'But, it's not working. Why is it not working?'

'How did you get this?' Patrick said, as he took the device from Engella's hand. He checked it carefully and tried to activate the device himself. 'It looks like the power's gone. Strange.'

'It's a long story. I'll tell you everything, but first I need your help with something.' She reached inside her backpack and retrieved her journal, flicking through the pages until she found the notes she'd made about the holocube. She checked her scribbles, and eventually found the text she had been looking for. 'Look at this ... right here. Do you know what this means?'

Patrick adjusted his spectacles and read the words aloud.

Keep going. We'll find you. ER.

α - β - γ - δ - ε

Graviton Dynamics
Where the past and future unite

Evergreen Gardens, New Shanghai City,
Asian Protectorate

'Where did you find this information?' Patrick asked, his expression one of complete surprise.

'It was contained in the holocube I showed you. My papa left it for me when I was a child. It's a message, but I'm not quite sure what it means.'

'You said he left it for you?' Patrick asked. 'Where did he leave it?'

'I found it in New Shanghai many years ago, when I was a little girl. I've been trying to work out what it means ever since.'

Patrick pointed towards Engella's wrist. 'Do you mind if I take a look at your shiftband?' he asked.

Engella reached out her hand and allowed Patrick to pull back her sleeve until her shiftband was visible. He pointed to the symbol, which Annys had pointed out previously.

'Beta,' she said. 'I understand the Greek letters correspond to the different shiftbands, the proto-types you developed with my parents. But I don't understand what the place name is for. I thought it could be where the other shiftbands are located, but without a timepoint it's impossible to know.'

Patrick nodded. 'I think I might be able to help you with that,' he said.

'You can?' Engella asked.

Patrick got up from the sofa and made his way over to the staircase. He removed a key from his top pocket, unlocked the door and reached inside to remove a large patterned box. He placed it on the tabletop and removed the lid. 'Have you ever consid-ered a career as a detective?' he asked, with a wide grin. 'That information you have. You're right, it was a message. But only part of it...'

He rustled through the box and removed two small silver cubes.

Engella gasped as she realised what they were.

'Your mother activated her shiftband and was about to hand me a shiftband too, but the Hunters attacked. Your mother made me leave through the wormhole she'd opened, so I did, but it collapsed before you and your parents could follow. Without a shiftband there was no way for me to make it back, and there was no way I could contact your parents for help.'

'I'm sorry,' Engella said.

'Before the attack, your mother and I had already stored the remaining shiftbands in a place where the Company wouldn't be able to find them. We were supposed to go and collect them before we left, but let's just say our plans didn't quite work out as we expected.'

'So, you know where the other shiftbands are?' Engella asked.

'Yes. We stored a map of the storage location in two holocubes. One holocube contained the location, and the other contained the exact timepoint. The message you received wasn't complete, Engella. You had the place, but you didn't have the right time. You need both holocubes to complete the message.'

Engella considered what she'd heard. It would be impossible to find the right timepoint now. 'So that's it then. I don't have any way of finding the other holocube. It's impossible.'

'Oh, I think you'll find that nothing is impossible, Engella,' Patrick said, smiling. 'I had both of them in my suitcase. I never gave one to your father. I have no idea who gave you yours, but it certainly wasn't

Evan.' He passed the holocubes to Engella.

'How is this possible? Engella asked, as she examined the reflective surfaces. She looked at her own holocube, weathered and scratched from age. She compared it to the others and realised she was holding the same holocube in her hands, but from different points in time.

'This looks like a temporal paradox to me,' said Patrick.

'I don't understand.'

'I'll give you some advice about trying to understand paradoxes ... don't even try.'

Engella understood there was no point in trying to understand. She was quite talented when it came to particle physics, but some things were even too difficult for an experienced theoretical physicist to process, let alone a relatively inexperienced seventeen-year-old. So she decided to let it go. Still, she was less concerned about the paradox and more upset by the discovery that the message may not have been from her father, after all. One thing brought her comfort, though – something she could now be sure about: 'I knew Annys had sent me here for a reason,' she said. 'Everything's all starting to make sense now.'

'Annys?' Patrick said, his eyes wide.

'She's my friend.'

Patrick nodded, without saying a word.

'Will you come with me?' Engella asked. 'To New Shanghai, I mean?'

Patrick shook his head. 'I can't,' he said. 'I have responsibilities here. Someone's counting on me. Besides, the Hunters would be on top of me in seconds. Your parents and I were the most wanted people in New Shanghai. I wouldn't make it down the first alley without a drone spotting me. You, on the other hand, can go wherever you want,' he said, as he pointed at her shiftband.

'That's true, but I have a problem. I'm not sure how I can go back to New Shanghai without the Hunters tracking me here. As soon as I shift, they'll come looking for me. I don't want to put you at risk ... The Lights of Time.'

'Ah yes,' Patrick said. 'Your mother's ...'

'— Theory...I guess we've proven her right.'

'Is there anything you don't know?' Patrick chuckled.

'I know a lot, thanks to my friend, Annys. She sent me here. That's how I found you.'

Patrick smiled. 'I see. How very curious. Can I see your holocube again?' he asked.

Engella passed it to Patrick who began tinkering

with the device. 'Hmmm. This isn't right,' he said.

'Hold on,' Engella said, as she reached inside her pocket and pulled out the inhibitor. 'I think it's something to do with this.'

'Ah, yes. That'll do it. That's HuntCorp tech. How on Earth did you get your hands on one of those?'

'Another long story,' Engella said, with a grin.

'There's one problem with your mother's theory, you see. It's a wonderful theory, don't get me wrong. Following quarks through space-time and moving between places and times and all that. But what happens when you switch off the lights?'

Engella shook her head, completely perplexed.

Patrick switched off the inhibitor, and they watched as the blue eye faded to black. 'You disappear,' he said. 'Try the holocube now...'

Engella waved her hand over the device and light burst outwards, illuminating the entire room.

'It's a technology inhibitor,' Patrick said. 'A brilliant piece of tech. Not my design, unfortunately. Let's put it back on, shall we? Just in case.' He reactivated the inhibitor, and they watched as the lights of the holocube faded out.

'Pretty cool, now I know how it works,' Engella said.

'You said the Hunters had been on your tail? Well,

all they'd managed to do was to track your tech. Use an inhibitor like this and the Lights of Time go out.'

The news was groundbreaking for Engella, as finally, after all these years, she had found a way to conceal herself from the Hunters. By using the inhibitor in between shifts, the Hunters would find it far more challenging to find her.

'Now, Engella, I'd like you to tell me everything. Go back to the beginning, when you lost your parents. What has happened to you since and who did you meet along the way? You mentioned someone called Annys earlier? I'd very much like to hear more about her, if that's okay.'

Engella nodded. 'Well, here goes,' she said. 'It all started eight years ago. My parents pushed me through a wormhole, and they were left behind. I was all alone in New Shanghai. But one day, I came across a holocube and it changed everything ...'

A few hours had passed since Engella had told Patrick her story. She sat on the sofa, and stared at the wood burner, as the last cinders of some firewood burned away. She couldn't believe what she had learned that day. Her mind was racing, as she'd finally found some of the answers she'd sought for so long. She closed her eyes and tried to clear her mind. She had made some important discoveries, and she still hadn't quite digested it all.

Patrick returned to the sitting room with his briefcase held out in front of him. He placed it on the table and clicked open the catch.

'Did you find it?' Engella asked.

Patrick smiled a warm smile. 'I sure did,' he said. He reached inside his open briefcase and pulled out a pile of photographs.

Engella took them in her hands and gripped them tightly, her hands shaking with anticipation. She gazed at the images and her eyes welled up. Her heart ached with grief.

Still. How wonderful it was to see their faces again. She began to cry and wiped the tears from her eyes.

Patrick looked away awkwardly, unsure whether he should comfort her or not. 'Are you okay?' he asked.

'Yes, I'm fine. I didn't think I'd ever see them again. How do these photos even exist? Everything else is gone. It's like they were deleted from history.'

'I've been thinking about everything you've told me. I think there may be more to space-time travel then we'd anticipated. We've already discovered one paradox. So, I guess this is another one for the list.'

Engella nodded, but she didn't really understand everything she'd heard. She looked at the photograph again. It had been taken in her parents' back garden, when they had lived in the Asian Protectorate during their post-graduate days. They'd taken the image in one of the biodomes, which was filled with tropical plants. It even had its own ecosystem, with wildlife: birds flapped in the trees while fishes sloshed about in the artificial river system which had been built into the walkways. Patrick stood proudly in the photo next to Evan Rhys and May Nakamura.

'Take it, Engella. It's yours.'

Engella wiped a tear away from her face. 'Thank you,' she said.

Engella had spent several hours telling Patrick about her life. He had seemed particularly interested in Annys, yet whenever Engella probed him about the reasons why, he was silent. He wasn't being completely open about everything, but Engella was satisfied that he'd tell her at the right time.

'I know what I need to do. But I'll be honest, I'm scared about it,' Engella said.

'I'm sorry I can't join you. I really am. You'd think I would leap at the chance to get back, especially after being stranded here. But to be honest, this is my home now. I can't imagine ever leaving,' Patrick said.

'I have everything I need now,' Engella said. 'Thanks to you. I guess there's nothing stopping me. I'll come back for you though, I promise.'

'Take both of these,' Patrick said, as he passed Engella the holocubes. 'You need them more than I do.'

Engella paused for a moment.

'What's wrong?' Patrick asked.

'It's my friend, Annys. She's in trouble. I need to help her. But I need to find the shiftbands first.'

'What happened to her?' Patrick said, his face concerned.

'The Hunters caught her,' Engella said. 'They took her away, I know where they've taken her, well, I think I do. I just need to figure out the right time-point, so I can go and rescue her.'

Patrick nodded. 'Your friend,' he said. 'Can you tell me more about her?'

Engella thought back to the first time she'd met Annys on the beach. She described everything she could remember from that day, until Patrick finally said something in reply. 'I know this may sound like a strange question, but how old is your friend?'

'Erm, do you know what? I don't know. We've

never discussed it. I'd guess she's in her early fifties? Why do you ask?' Engella said.

'I'm just curious,' Patrick said, as he looked to the floor. He placed his hand on his chin, as though he was contemplating something. He nodded to himself, mumbled a few words and finally turned to face Engella again. 'Okay, we need to formulate a plan. You have all the details. You know the time and place, so you can shift there. I think you can reach the storage location and be back again in a few hours. It's not going to be easy, so you need to prepare for every eventuality.'

'Let's get started,' Engella said.

They talked for hours, and both scrawled out notes on papers which were laid out across the table. Patrick described the different routes which could be taken to the storage location. They reviewed the maps which had been hidden within the holocubes, which Engella copied out by hand into her journal.

By now, Patrick had shared every nugget of information he could possibly think of to help Engella on her mission. 'You'll need this,' he said, as he scrawled down a passcode on a sheet of paper. 'You'll need this code to access the storage box.'

Engella nodded and placed the paper in her pocket. She was now as prepared as she was going to be.

'As soon as I leave,' Engella said, 'Activate the inhibitor. I don't want you getting any visitors before I return.'

Patrick nodded. 'All I need to do is switch it off and on again. Even if you're gone for days, you'll find yourself back here moments later.'

Engella prepared to activate her shiftband. 'See you soon,' she said.

'Safe journey,' Patrick replied. 'Are you ready to finish what your mother and I started?'

A year passed, and so did another.

Eddie sat at his laptop in the dark, his bedroom partially lit by the code which flickered across his screen.

He'd lived with his foster parents in Socorro for over a year now, after spending some time in care. They'd been good to him, and they cared for him deeply. He was happy there – as happy as he could have been, really, considering what he'd been through – but he still missed his old home in Truth or Consequences.

It had taken him months to settle into the new town; he'd struggled to cope with the dramatic changes to his life. But with time, and with a lot of patience from his foster parents, he was able to get there in the end. He'd immersed himself in his studies – his mom would have wanted it that way and, as he'd always had an interest in computer science, he'd decided to take it as his major. It wasn't long before he'd excelled; his talents for using technology outdid the other members of his class by miles. He'd become bored with always being one step ahead of the other students, so he immersed himself in a number of extra-curricular activities.

Secretly, he'd learned how to access the dark web, where his learning had escalated exponentially, and by now he'd become a talented hacker by the name of Cypher-16.

Everything he'd done up until that day, and everything he'd worked towards since the day his mother had died was for one purpose, and one purpose only. He'd made it his mission to find out who had killed his mother.

He ripped open the envelope, which had been stamped with HuntCorp's official seal, and pulled out the letter; almost ripping it in his haste. He scanned the page and didn't stop reading until he'd finished.

'I'm in,' he said, smiling, although his happiness was bittersweet. His attempts to hack the mainframe via the dark web had been successful. He'd accessed the files which listed data on the new recruits who had joined the Company. It wasn't long before he was able to add a new entry to the database. At sixteen, Eddie was now old enough to register for the security patrol, so he was able to approve his own application with relative ease. It hadn't taken a lot, really. All he'd had to do was to create a false personnel file, adding essential biological data – fingerprints, iris scans – and a photograph too.

The Huntington Corporation had expanded its operations considerably since they had purchased the old military base, and their compound was now a bustling metropolis.

He held the letter of approval like it was some kind of trophy. Once inside, he'd use his experience as a hacker to access the central servers and find out exactly who was allocated to the Hunters' patrol on that fateful day.

The day which changed his life forever.

He wouldn't stop until he'd found the person responsible.

He just needed to get inside the compound, and now he'd found a way.

β ⊝

2066-OCT-24 07:01

NEW SHANGHAI CITY, ASIAN PROTECTORATE

The vortex swirled into a whirlwind and the portal slammed shut. Engella checked her surroundings, and quickly ducked into a nearby passageway when she realised she'd materialised among the market stalls of a bustling street. Papers floated about on the air-flows and crumpled aluminium cans tumbled around the ground. Space-time returned to normal, and the passageway was calm again.

She watched the sky until she was sure there were no drones hovering in the vicinity. The street lights hanging above swung on the breeze, creaking as they moved. They shone a deep, warm orange in the empty street. They were Chinese lanterns, so Engella knew instantly that she was in the right place. Once she was satisfied that the coast was clear, she explored the passageway to identify all of the possible escape routes. She did this silently and quickly – it had been her nature to do so for so many years now, after all.

Beads of sweat formed on her forehead as the humidity of the city warmed her to uncomfortable levels. Her adrenaline peaked, and she began to calm herself again. She'd almost expected a gang of Hunters to fall out of a portal at any minute, but with each moment that passed she became more at ease. Without the inhibitor she was open to attack again. The Hunters had multiple ways to find her in this place and time. Of course, they could discover her quark trail, but they also had access to the city's vast communications network. Facial recognition, in particular, was her enemy. She pulled her hood over her head and concealed her plaited hair. She kept her head down, and only looked up when absolutely necessary. All the Hunters required was a photograph of her face which would be used to scan and measure her facial dimensions. The data would flash up on their systems almost instantly, as the AI programmes - used to analyse the image - alerted the authorities.

Engella noted a camera had been placed in between

the passageway and the main street ahead, scanning people as they passed by. She'd need to duck down, and make sure her image would not be registered. She lifted the collar on her jacket higher and pulled her hood down further, to conceal as much of her face as possible. She edged along the wall and could now see the bustling crowds which zigzagged between the market stalls. The scent of spices drifted in the air and the stalls were stocked to the brink with different varieties of fruit, vegetables, and herbs.

The market was familiar. Engella had been there before, but she couldn't remember exactly when it was. She had searched the streets many times in the past but finally, this time, she had a clear mission ahead of her. She had a new purpose. She knew exactly where – and when – she needed to be. But the reality of the task ahead still overwhelmed her. Moving through the city undetected would almost be impossible. But she had to try her best. Annys, and Patrick too, were counting on her.

Engella opened her journal and read the pages. She'd made a sketch of the map, which she'd copied directly from the projection of both holocubes. This was the sensible thing to do, as there was a risk that the projections from the holocubes would get unwanted attention.

ᴈ β

Since Engella and her parents were separated, the Hunters had continued to erase all evidence of their existence. Engella had searched for clues about their whereabouts for many years, and she'd wondered how many times she'd been on the brink of finding out something important. Had she ever been close to finding some piece of crucial information about them, for it to be wiped – deleted from history – with only seconds to spare? Her mind wandered. There was no point in dwelling on it now. She'd never know the truth, anyway. She finally had some useful information, which had been contained in the two holocubes.

Engella reached inside her pocket and removed the photograph of her parents. She still gasped when she saw it and was still reeling from its discovery. It gave her a level of comfort she'd not felt for years. However dreadful things became from now on, the photograph would help get her through it. She could see their faces again whenever she wanted, and couldn't believe how good it made her feel. Thanks to Patrick, everything was much clearer now.

She darted to the end of the passageway and dodged around a damaged refuse-bot which was obviously confused, as it repeatedly bumped its head against the wall.

As she reached the market she could see crowds of people of all shapes and sizes as they wandered among the stalls. An elderly woman dressed in a brightly coloured gown held a watermelon between her hands, squeezing it to see how ripe it was. A young man was in the middle of a chilli-sauce tasting session, as sauces of various hotness were passed to him by the stallholder. He eventually decided upon a glowing, red sauce which looked almost radioactive, and after only tasting a tiny drop, he gasped and ran to the nearest water fountain to put out the flames in his mouth. He raised his fist towards the stallholder and shouted something rather rude.

A band of street performers juggled with metallic-looking balls, dancing as they meandered their way through the crowds. Passers-by cheered and clapped, until the performers reached out for donations, at which point they lost interest. The performers held out their hats eagerly, hoping to receive at least a few credits for their time and effort. Next, Engella laughed at a poor magician who tried the 'pull-a-rabbit-out-of-a-robot' trick – only to reveal, by accident it seemed, that the poor animal had been stuffed under his coat the whole time.

Engella checked her hood to ensure her face was

concealed and moved into the sea of people. She found herself pushing against the tide, as more and more people flooded into the market, until at one point it was almost impossible to move at all. Engella felt anxious, her exits blocked.

She gazed at the vast cityscape which towered above. Lines of hovercars and shuttles chugged across the sky as they carried passengers between the different levels of the city, their propulsion systems spewing out gases from their exhausts which left little trails in between the clouds.

Engella admired the sheer height of the city's domes; the upper levels vanishing into the cloudline. But she didn't have time for sightseeing. She felt exposed. It was essential that she found shelter as soon as possible. She knew the market would only get busier as the morning progressed, so she knew she had to move elsewhere. She pushed her way further through the crowd and passed a stall which was serving seafood, then held back – the smell of the grilled lobster making her mouth water. Her stomach rumbled and she realised she hadn't eaten for a while.

After ducking inside a side street, she removed her journal to check her map. She wasn't sure exactly where she was until she came across a very helpful road sign, which confirmed her exact location and showed her where she was with respect to the nearest transport hub. The road sign also asked Engella how her day had been going and told her about his plans for the weekend too.

Engella estimated how long it would be until she reached the storage location. She calculated that she still had a considerable walk ahead before she reached the transport hub which linked the middle and upper domes.

Eventually, she reached one of the city's parks, and noticed an empty bench with a view of the harbour and the East China Sea.

The bench was perfectly placed: not only could she see far out to sea, but she also had a panoramic view of the New Shanghai City Metropolis. The last time she'd seen the three domes of the city so close was when she was in the Yixing Forest with Annys.

She couldn't shake the final image of her friend from her mind. But she managed to refocus, flicking through her journal to confirm the best route for her to take, one which Patrick had advised was the safest possible.

It was time for her to travel into the domes above. Incredibly risky, due to the additional levels of security of the high-levs, but essential to her mission. She scanned the harbour and docks, until she found the transport hub.

She approached a cluster of people, remembering to keep her head down as much as possible. It was likely that the transport hub would have additional security – bio-scanners and security-bots – so she kept her eyes peeled.

At first she just watched other people from afar as they tapped on the consoles, before they climbed inside their pod and then disappeared in a puff of light, only to reappear somewhere else within the city.

Engella finally got the courage to join the queue of travellers, and it wasn't long before she was near to the front. She checked the screen in preparation but was distressed to discover that the control panel required some sort of biological identification to activate, either a fingerprint or an iris scan.

Anxious not to provide any biometric data, Engella hesitated. A bio-scan would be an ideal way for the Hunters to track her through space-time. The data would flood into cyberspace within seconds, and it wouldn't be long before an AI algorithm had tracked her down. Spies were everywhere, and they were often hidden in plain sight like an invisible trap, ready to swing shut at any moment.

Engella considered her next move and allowed the next person in line to take her place.

And then, she saw them – beams of orange light, which hovered across the harbour. She relaxed once she realised there was an easier way to travel.

A little further down the harbour, another queue of people waited to board holo-platforms. They were much slower than the transport pods, but they didn't appear to have the same level of security. Engella watched as the glowing boards glided across the harbour in different directions, before lifting off into the city above.

Engella joined the back of the queue, and was pleased to find that it was much shorter than the one she'd just been in. A short Maori woman with the most exquisite facial tattoo waited patiently in front. Her large patterned shopping bag wobbled about, and Engella was certain she could hear it growling at her. She peered inside to see a tiny genetically modified lion cub looking back. The animal grumbled then let out a little growl, before raising its front paws and swinging them wildly towards Engella.

The woman turned around. 'Good morning, don't you worry, darling. She won't bite. In fact, I think she likes you.' She proceeded to lift the animal out of her shopping bag and held the cub closely. The lion was tiny – probably only a fifth of the size of a wild-born animal. The cub licked the woman's hand and nuzzled her neck, before curling into a fluffy ball.

'May I?' Engella asked, as she reached out to pat the cub on the head.

'Go ahead,' the woman said, 'But watch your fingers.' She chuckled as Engella withdrew her hand, only to realise quite quickly that the woman had been joking.

Engella lifted the animal from the woman's arms. The cub tried to wrestle away until Engella held her close, stroking her head. She could feel the cub's growl reverberate through her body, eventually turning to a purr. She realised this was the closest she'd ever been to a lion before, and she'd never dreamed she would hold one. The cub finally settled and began to lick Engella's hand.

Engella giggled. 'It tickles,' she said. She placed her hand on the cub's head, making her purr like a kitten. 'She's lovely. Where did you get her?'

'You know, from CLONEPETZ,' the woman said. 'It's one of those GenMod stores, over in the shopping district.'

Engella thought back – she was sure she'd seen a

GenMod store before. The laws surrounding genetic modification, or 'GenMod' as it later became known, were relaxed across the Protectorate in the late 2050s. People didn't only modify their pets, but they also modified themselves too, if they had enough cash to pay for it, of course. Initially, people only had minor alterations, such as a change to their eye colour or hair type. Nonetheless, it wasn't long before they'd started to take it to the extreme and the GenMod craze was truly born. There had been stories of how some people had even had animal genes incorporated into their own genome. There was always somebody trying to cause a stir and be the talk of the town as they showed off their brand-new zebra stripes, their chameleon-like skin tone or their lustrous lion's mane.

Engella handed the cub back to the woman. 'I'd love to get one myself,' she said.

'Oh, honey, it's really easy and not too expensive anymore, if you're happy with a copy that is. It's only the unique, made-to-order animals that cost a bomb.'

'A copy? How does that work?'

'Why bother paying for a unique animal to be grown up, when you can choose one you already like and copy its DNA? Far cheaper. You just need a replication pack. They're only twenty credits each.'

Engella thought about it. 'How does it work?' she asked.

'You just need to take a sample of DNA of the animal you want and the guys in the store grow it up for you. It only takes a couple of hours.'

'Thanks for the tip,' said Engella.

'Check this out,' the woman said. 'I had Charlie modified, but I added in a few extras. Did you know that squid have luminous genes?'

'In fact, yes I did!'

'Take a look at this, then.'

The woman reached inside her pocket and pulled out a bunch of keys, moving them around until she found her keyring, which had a small torch attached. She clicked on the switch and shone the beam directly into the cub's face. Her eyes glowed a bright luminous green.

'Woah,' said Engella.

'I had her vision upgraded. Not only does she see better, but she also glows in the dark! Fabulous at parties.' The woman tickled the cub which made her growl again. She placed her back into her shopping bag, and the lion curled up inside. 'Anyway, looks like my holo-platform's here. It was great to chat. Have a good day!'

'You too!' said Engella. She patted the cub on the head one last time and said her goodbyes. She'd fallen in love with the little fluff-ball. Maybe she'd be able to afford her own, one day.

She stepped back and watched the woman who, with her pet cub in hand, boarded the holo-platform. It hovered close to the ground until the woman had stepped on and had been safely secured.

The holo-platforms alternated as they rotated, each one travelling in a unique direction. While some crossed the harbour, others moved vertically: shooting upwards with great speed.

Engella waited for her own holo-platform to dock and prepared to step aboard. As her feet touched down, she was surprised at how sturdy it was – especially as the platform was only made of a combination of photons and lasers. Once she'd boarded, the whole system started to hum. The floor glowed white before turning an intense orange.

'Good morning, traveller. I hope you're having a wonderful day,' the holo-platform said, in a high-pitched robotic voice. 'Please confirm your destination.'

'Oh, hello, I'd like to erm...' Engella suddenly realised she hadn't yet considered the route she'd need to take via the holo-platforms. Most of the route she'd noted down in her journal had been all via foot. 'Erm, go over to the harbour please ... erm, no, wait ... take me to the upper levels.'

'Please specify an exact location,' the holo-platform continued.

'Okay, err ... take me to the nearest GenMod store.' It was the first thing that came to mind.

Engella pulled out her journal and checked the map, and quickly memorised the names of the surrounding streets.

'What's the nearest drop-off location to the Middle Dome Archiving District?'

'Thank you for your confirmation,' the holo-platform said as it jolted forwards before accelerating into the air. Engella almost lost her footing, but she was quickly held in place by a vivid yellow protective force-field, which cushioned her like a cubed-shaped bubble.

'Time to destination: Eighteen minutes,' the holo-platform said. 'Would you like to listen to some music while you wait?'

Engella nodded. 'Erm, okay. Go on then.' The holo-platform was suddenly filled with the wails and screams of a New Shanghai Techno-Rapper, who sounded as if he was in pain rather than performing a piece of music. Engella covered her ears.

'Something else, please!' Engella yelled over the racket. 'And quieter, too!'

The holo-platform changed the track to a piece of classical music instead – Bach, if Engella remembered correctly – and adjusted the volume until it was at a more acceptable level. Once Engella was comfortable, she sat down on a holographic chair which had materialised in the centre of the floor. She settled, and even began to enjoy the trip. She looked down at her feet to see the ground falling away. For a moment she felt a little dizzy, so she closed her eyes and focused on the music instead.

Glad I'm not scared of heights.

The panorama of the city around her was an incredible sight. She passed another transport hub – this time on one of the higher levels – and she could see multiple holo-platforms as they accelerated away. Some disappeared into the clouds above, while others zoomed past on a similar trajectory as her own, each filled with people who were going about their days: an elderly couple with a speckled-brown Dachshund in one, and a father and a young boy in another. Engella could see the boy was holding a rather bulky robot with a metallic screen for a face, which was almost as big as he was.

Soon she'd approached the middle dome of the

city, which was so high up she'd already moved past the cloud line.

This is high. Really high. I'm, erm... Not scared of heights. Engella hoped that the more she told herself this, the more she'd believe it. It didn't seem to be working.

The holo-platform continued its journey as it zoomed across the sky. Engella observed the other platforms. They were quite beautiful from this distance, glistening in the morning sun like fireflies who had got their times all wrong. As the holo-platform approached the docking level, Engella watched the others as they slowed and reached the dock, pausing momentarily for the people to step outside.

Engella's holo-platform shuddered before beginning to climb again. By now the view was truly remarkable. Engella could see all three domes of the floating city, and could make out small points of black dotting the horizon. They were approaching her direction rapidly and she realised they were delivery-drones, transferring food and other purchases to the rows of apartments above.

The holo-platform shuddered again – stronger this time – and enough to rock Engella from her seat. At first she was startled but the judder subsided, so Engella assumed it was just air turbulence.

All of a sudden the holo-platform slowed to a halt, before accelerating upwards at maximum speed.

Engella gasped and held to the chair tightly as the judders increased in intensity.

'Please can you slow down?' Engella asked, now feeling uneasy. There was no reply. 'Hello...? Is there anybody there?'

The high-pitched robotic voice stuttered a reply. 'Unable to pppppppppprocess.' The voice continued to warp and slowed until it was barely audible.

'Unab-b-b-b-b ...'

The classical music was suddenly replaced by a glaring roar.

Engella covered her ears and winced in pain. She managed to turn her head just enough to see the city's promenades rush past as the holo-platform hurtled higher at a terrifying speed.

And then, as suddenly as it had rushed away, the holo-platform came to a screeching halt, knocking Engella to her knees. Luckily, the force of the rapid change in direction was subdued by the holographic stabilisers which, fortunately for Engella, were still functional – although only just.

Engella gripped the chair tightly, her breathing rapid. Once she was certain the holo-platform still had a floor, she peered over the edge to discover the awful truth that she was hundreds of metres higher than she was supposed to be – now almost parallel to the highest levels of the upper dome. There was something wrong with the system, and the lights began to fade. Small cracks forked their way through the chair, like broken glass in a shattered mirror. If the holo-platform malfunction worsened and the platform disappeared completely, there was no chance she'd survive the fall.

I've been in situations like this before. I can do this.

There was no harm in trying the system again, to see if she could reboot it. 'Hello?' she said, calmly. 'Please take me to my destination. I'm ready to get off, now.'

There was no reply.

Okay. That didn't work.

Engella's neck prickled. She reached for her holster and pulled out her blaster ready to respond if the need arose. She waited in silence and checked her vantage points. Had the Hunters hacked the holo-platform's system? And, more importantly, was she now at their mercy?

Engella observed the horizon and could now make out several objects far off into the distance, approaching at high speed.

At first, Engella assumed that they were transport pods, but transport pods didn't often travel this high. She squinted, covering her eyes from the glaring sun, and tried to make out what they were.

They were coming, and they were coming in fast.

The realisation of what was approaching hit Engella like a freight train. She frantically checked the cabin and looked for any way she could release herself, but there was no way out.

She reached for her shiftband. The only escape for her now was to undertake a high-altitude shift: but a shift at this height was perilous and possibly deadly.

Still. She didn't have time to decide, as the military-grade drones were already upon her.

She watched in horror as the drones activated their targeting systems, each one aiming its bulky cannon at her.

She tried to activate her shiftband, but it all happened too fast.

The drones fired their lasers, each one propelling a red streak of terror tearing across the sky.

Engella felt like the world had slowed down, and all she could do was watch.

This time, she thought, there would be no escape.

Annys drifted into consciousness. She tried to open her eyes, but she was too weak. She could hear something – voices, perhaps. She couldn't tell. She tried to focus on the sounds, but her head was too fuzzy. Finally, she opened her eyes to see strip lights streaming overhead.

The sounds were clearer now. They *were* voices. Two men in white hospital gowns marched alongside her, accompanying her magno-bed as it floated along the spotless corridor.

Annys tried to move her head, but realised her neck had been put in a brace. She managed to turn her head just enough to see rooms as they streamed past, their large glass windows reflecting the fluorescent lights.

She thought back to the events which had led her to this point. Her last memory was being captured and telling Engella to leave, watching as she escaped through a portal. Now it all made sense. She was a prisoner within a Hunter base, and she was about to be 'processed', as the Hunters liked to call it.

She could hear distant screams from elsewhere, somewhere deep within the facility – other prisoners experiencing a similar fate, perhaps.

They reached the corridor's end, when the bed ploughed into the closed doors, sending them crashing open. Annys was almost fully awake by now; the Hunters' tranquiliser wearing off.

'Where... Where are you taking me?' Annys managed to say but her voice was quiet, and her words slurred.

They were now inside a large room which looked as though it was used for clinical procedures.

Annys found it hard to stay awake and closed her eyes again. She opened her eyes just in time to see the surgeons on either side as they wielded their weapons above her.

Annys had heard the terrible stories of the Hunters and their memory extraction techniques.

The surgeon reached over Annys and made the first incision into her neck.

Annys cried out, but there was no sound.

She closed her eyes again, but this time she'd passed out from the pain.

2066-OCT-24 10:14

NEW SHANGHAI CITY, ASIAN PROTECTORATE

The explosions lit up the sky, like an erratic firework display which had been let off by mistake. The fireball eventually subsided to reveal a tangled mass of hundreds of pieces of charred and twisted metal drifting downwards.

Engella stood rigid, still in shock, her hands still shaking.

She watched as the last pieces of the destroyed drones fell away.

All except one, that was. A single drone remained, the one responsible for the carnage, the one who'd committed the most cardinal sin against its brethren.

The drone's single eye blinked. Engella watched

it anxiously, expecting it to turn on her too. But it didn't; it just hovered there with a trail of smoke still oozing from its cannon, glowing red-hot from the blast.

The drone tried several times to reboot but it didn't have much success. It appeared to be jammed.

Something had gone terribly wrong – for the drones that was. Engella was rather pleased with the outcome and wasn't complaining at all.

The machine appeared to have experienced a malfunction, and a critical one at that. After it had blown its siblings out of the sky, it just hovered like a confused bird, unsure what to do next.

Engella could now hear the hum of a holo-platform, as it hurtled towards her. 'What now?' she yelled, as she held her head in preparation for the impending collision.

As had been the case with her own rapid ascent, the second holo-platform halted, but this one stopped a few metres above her. There was a person inside – she could see the shadow of their feet through the bottom of the holo-platform's semi-translucent floor.

Engella raised her blaster and prepared for the Hunter's attack, but seconds passed, and before long a whole minute had gone by in which nothing had happened at all. She heard a crash, and she was surprised to see that the remaining drone had suddenly lost all power. Its four propellers had stalled, and it tumbled downwards like a stone.

The second holo-platform suddenly jolted upwards and disappeared from sight.

Engella's own holo-platform rumbled before jolting forwards on its journey again.

The familiar and now rather comforting voice of the holo-platform returned: 'I apologise for the delay,' the holo-platform said. 'We're currently experiencing technical difficulties.'

'You think?' Engella blurted out. 'Tell me about it.'

'Time to destination: twelve minutes,' the holo-platform said, before it returned to its original flight-plan – this time, at a much more pleasant speed.

The holo-platform played Bach over the speakers again and Engella sat back down in her holographic chair.

She didn't have the foggiest idea what had just happened.

The holo-platform arrived at the middle dome, and finally docked at level twenty-eight.

'You'll find the nearest GenMod store in bay forty-nine,' the holo-platform said.

'Thanks,' said Engella.

'I hope you enjoyed your journey, please come again.'

'Uh, no thanks,' Engella said, as she disembarked. 'I'll take the stairs next time.'

2021-APR-17 13:44

COMPOUND, OUTSIDE TRUTH OR CONSEQUENCES, NEW MEXICO, UNITED STATES OF AMERICA

Annys was awoken by a series of bangs, clangs, and the occasional scream from somewhere else within the prison. She could hardly see a thing, as the cell was pitch-black, except for a tiny slit of light which made it through under the door. She felt woozy, and grabbed her temples to ease her throbbing head. She'd been knocked out by something far stronger this time – probably another type of enhanced tranquiliser liquid; one of the Hunters' special concoctions.

Even though Annys now found herself in a dire situation, she managed to smile in the knowledge that she'd sent Engella somewhere safe. That, after all, was all that mattered. A special person would be waiting there for Engella, and Annys was absolutely certain that he wouldn't let them down.

After the vortex had closed, Annys had been tied up and forced into an armoured vehicle. She remembered the pain she'd felt as they placed a needle into her neck. Probably her first dose of tranquilliser.

The locking mechanism of the cell door clunked and the door opened slightly, just enough to flood the room with light. Annys covered her face from the glare, and it took a few moments for her eyes to adjust. She could see two shadows as they entered through the doorway.

'Lights!' Tala yelled, her speech activating the strip lights above.

'Camera! Action?' Annys said with a slight smirk.

Tala stared at Annys blankly. She was either not impressed with sarcasm or she hadn't understood the joke.

'Welcome to your new home,' Lera said. 'I hope you're prepared for an extended stay.'

'Oh, it's lovely dear, thank you,' Annys said. 'Although, where's my upgrade?' Her voice was hoarse and dry. She hadn't had any water for hours, and the tranquillisers she'd received hadn't helped the situation.

She checked the doorway and two guards stepped inside; one stationed on each side of the door. They wore black fitted body-suits with shiny black helmets, and their visors covered most of their faces, with only their mouths visible.

'Do you even know what kind of damage you've done?' said Tala.

Annys looked her straight in the eyes and just stared at her, unwilling to reply at first. But the sight of the Hunter who'd attacked her at her cottage in Skye infuriated Annys so much that she couldn't help but say something. 'Damage to the Company, don't you mean? I'm so glad I was able to help,' she said defiantly.

'It's taken us years to repair the timeline,' Lera snapped. 'It's in everyone's best interests if you just tell us where the remaining shiftbands are – and Engella too, for that matter. We'll find them anyway, so you may as well help. That way, you may see the light of day again.'

'Who's Engella?' Annys said. 'Never heard of her.'

'Don't play the idiot,' Tala snarled.

Lera pulled out a holocube and activated the device, until a three-dimensional image shined brightly on the cell's walls. It was a high-definition photograph of Engella and Annys as they stood outside the fence of the compound.

'Sightseeing, were you?' Lera asked.

Annys shook her head. 'Oh, sorry dear, you meant *that* Engella!'

'Enough of the games!' Tala had snapped by this point, as rage bubbled up inside her. She placed both of her hands around Annys's neck and gripped it tightly. She tightened her hold and watched, grinning, as Annys began to choke.

'Commander?' said Lera, concerned by Tala's actions.

Tala turned and glared at Lera, before finally releasing Annys from her grip.

Annys spluttered, and after managing to take a few breaths, was able to get out a few words: 'I'll never tell you,' she said.

'We have evidence you've helped a known criminal traverse the space-time continuum,' Tala said. 'That's an instant life sentence.' She pointed towards Lera and then proceeded to pat her on the back. 'Thanks to this talented individual, that is.'

'We'll be on her tail by this time tomorrow,' said Lera. 'It won't be long before she's in the cell next door, so you may as well tell us what we want to know.'

'You'll never find her,' said Annys, her face defiant. 'I've made sure of it.'

Tala inched forwards and raised her hand, ready to strike Annys, but Lera interjected.

'Commander,' Lera said. 'This is against protocol.'

Tala scowled and pulled back her hand. A communicator crackled and Lera stepped back towards the door of the cell and whispered into the device. Annys tried to listen in, but she was too far away so she couldn't make it out.

Lera ended the conversation quickly and returned to the interrogation. 'Commander, you're needed in the command centre,' she said.

Tala's face was red with anger. So red, in fact, that her cheeks matched her curls of red hair. 'Carry on, recruit,' she said, as she bounded towards the door. 'Don't stop until you have answers.' She turned to Annys. 'See you soon,' she said with a wicked grin, before finally marching out of the room.

Lera acknowledged this with a nod and waited in silence until the commander had left the cell. She turned to face Annys, who had finally recovered from her ordeal. 'It's in your interest to cooperate,' she said. 'Be assured we take prisoner safety very seriously. You won't be harmed while under my care.'

'Forgive me if I don't believe you,' Annys said. 'But I'd rather trust actions rather than words.'

'You have to understand,' said Lera. 'I may not always agree with her methods, but she's a strong-willed commander who always puts the Company's interests first.'

'Even above people's lives?'

'You're the one who made it personal for Tala.'

'I assume you're referring to the moment when I blasted her at close range, no?'

'Possibly.'

'Well, in my defence, she did try to blow me up with a shock-grenade first. So I call it even.'

Lera leaned in closer to Annys. 'Just cooperate. It'll be easier for you that way,' she said.

Annys just stared forwards, more determined than ever to stand her ground.

'So, who are you, anyway?' Lera asked. 'And why are you helping Engella? What's in it for you?'

'I'm not going to tell you anything, so you may as well not even bother.'

'You've only just appeared on the timeline. Where have you been all these years? And why are you suddenly involved in all of this now? We know you helped Engella escape.'

Annys stayed silent. She was thinking on her feet and then opened her mouth to speak, before pausing again.

'Yes?' Lera asked.

'If my memory serves me correctly,' said Annys. 'I've never been involved in any crimes. I don't believe you have any grounds to hold me here.'

'That's not true. You're travelling through space-time without the authorisation of HuntCorp,' said Lera.

'Oh, I didn't realise the Company owned the whole of the space-time continuum,' Annys said, her tone now even more sarcastic than before.

'Until you understand the impact of this technology, you can't be trusted with its use. You have used it, haven't you?'

Annys looked at Lera in the eye. 'Maybe. Once or twice,' she said.

'I knew it,' said Lera.

'So, imagine for a moment that I agree to your demands, and I tell you the location of these so-called shiftbands you're looking for, if I knew where they were, of course. What would you actually do with them?'

'We'll destroy them,' Lera said, bluntly.

'So, you're saying the Company won't use the technology for its own advantage?'

Lera glared at Annys. 'We've already copied the research, we don't need it anymore.'

'But they're not perfect, are they? Your shift-bands, I mean.'

'I'm not telling you anything about our operations,' said Lera, as her expression went darker. 'Our tech works just fine. But I'm sure the prototypes would add additional functionalities that we may not have considered yet.'

'Thought so,' said Annys. 'What will come next? I suppose you'll sell them to the highest bidder?'

'HuntCorp would never share our technology.'

'Your technology? The shiftbands belong to Evan Rhys, May Nakamura and Patrick Munro. You stole the designs from them.'

'The Company bought them out. They have no right to hold the technology anymore. But anyway, that's irrelevant now. Once we're in complete control of every single shiftband, we'll make sure we make full use of their commercial potential.'

'To make money, you mean. That's all you care about.'

'Let's get back to the point, shall we?' said Lera. 'Your name ... now'

Annys shook her head, then grinned widely, once she'd realised she had the upper hand. 'If you don't know who I am...' she said. 'Then you clearly haven't been able to track us through space-time for as long as you said you did.'

'Have it your way,' Lera snapped. 'We'll hold you here permanently, so you can't cause any more damage to the timeline. It's that simple.'

'But as I understand it, everything is pre-determined. Hawking's theory about time travel showed us how events in the past are locked. We can't change them, as they've already happened. How will keeping me here make any difference?'

'Yes, that's right, to a degree. But the Company prefers that you're dealt with now. We'll edit the timeline and remove all of the damage that you and that renegade friend of yours did – one timepoint at a time. Anyone linked to you will be incarcerated, or worse.'

'Worse?'

'How about deletion?'

Annys's neck prickled. She thought about Patrick. He'd done so much for her. He didn't deserve to be hunted down and erased.

'Okay. I'll cooperate. But tell me one thing first.

Why does Tala have so much hate towards us?'

'You know I won't say. It's against everything we stand for. There are ...'

'Rules. Yes, dear, I know.'

'We won't let you follow this path of destruction anymore. But I can say this. Tala, well ... she's damaged. Things happened to her which changed her.'

'What path of destruction? We've hardly been anywhere,' Annys said, unsure what Lera was referring to.

'The attack...' Lera said. 'On New Shanghai.'

Annys was completely perplexed. 'Attack? I'm sorry, dear, but I honestly don't know what you're talking about.'

'Engella has blood on her hands and as you're her accomplice, so do you.'

Annys looked down at the ground. She tried to imagine what could have made the Hunter so full of hate. It must have been something terrible. 'I think you'd better check over this so-called evidence you have. It was probably tampered with ... to frame us.'

'Whatever the Company's faults,' Lera said. 'It would never falsify data. I accept some of our techniques are, well, a little severe sometimes, but the Company would never lie.'

'Ha! I see your brainwashing is well and truly complete,' Annys said.

Lera didn't know how to take this, as she honestly believed what she was saying. It occurred to her that she was spouting the Company's tagline like she'd memorised it from heart.

Annys continued. 'And if you only call my treatment here severe, I wouldn't like to see what you'd do to me on a *really* unpleasant day.'

Lera was the one who was now silent. Annys's words had clearly had an impact, and one of the guards seemed as though he'd noticed. He grunted in order to get Lera's attention.

Annys noticed, and gestured towards him. 'And another thing,' she said. 'You seriously need to have a good hard look at your recruitment policy. Do all of your agents come from the dregs of society?'

The guard who'd tried to get Lera's attention was particularly angered by Annys's comment, whereas the other one looked as though he was trying not to laugh.

'Present company excluded, of course,' Annys said, directing the comment towards Lera.

'How do I say this...? Our work requires a certain type of employee. Not everyone is willing to do the things we need them to. But it's for the good of the people.'

'It's always for the good of the people,' Annys said, with an icy stare. 'And you? How did you get involved in all of this? You seem far too good to be working with the likes of them.' Annys gestured towards the guard again, who coughed so violently in response that a little drop of spittle flicked across the room.

Annys raised her eyes in disgust.

'I believe in a better future,' Lera said. 'The misuse of this technology would be disastrous, especially in the wrong hands. People, places, and events literally wiped out of existence … and history changed forever.'

'I think you'll find it's already in the wrong hands – HuntCorp's,' Annys said. 'And talking about deletion … isn't that exactly what you've been doing? What about Evan Rhys? And May Nakamura? You've wiped them from history.'

'A means to an end,' said Lera.

Annys shook her head. 'Hypocrites.'

Lera moved closer to Annys, and looked straight into her eyes, although Annys didn't feel threatened this time, like she did when Tala interrogated her.

'Tell us everything,' Lera said. 'And we can repair it all. We'll erase the damage. And then you'll be sent to a maximum-security prison. You'll get a life sentence, of course.'

'What's the alternative?'

The grunting guard's radio buzzed. Lera looked up, and he summoned her over. The guard whispered something into her ear which made her smile.

'Well...' Lera said. 'That changes everything. The alternative? How about complete deletion? For you and all of your family.'

'My family? You'll never find them,' said Annys.

Lera glared at Annys. 'Really?' she asked. 'Are you sure about that, Annika?'

Annys gulped. She hadn't heard that name in years. She looked into Lera's eyes and for the first time, she experienced real fear.

'Good work, dear,' Annys said. 'You appear to know more about me than I realised...'

Engella journeyed deep into the city's streets until she eventually reached a busy plaza with a bubbling fountain in the centre. Street vendors manned their stalls on all sides, while their customers sat at tables and chairs which had been placed in line with the water's edge. Server-bots with unicycle-like wheels zipped around in all directions as they took customer orders, and then quite soon afterwards delivered their food to them. Engella was impressed with their efficiency.

The place was noisy too; filled with the clatter of pots and pans and the sizzles of food as it was cooked.

The aroma of several delicious creations drifted

upon the breeze and it didn't take long before Engella's stomach rumbled again. She sat down at the nearest vacant table and watched as several server-bots completed an impressive show of gymnastics to avoid hurtling into each other. She listened to an elderly man who was sat on the table next to her as he ordered his meal in Cantonese. The bot immediately got to work, its multiple arms flailing around, and grabbed a selection of ripe-looking vegetables. After a careful balancing act with a stack of plates, the bot pulled a wok away from its Tri-key to reveal a plate full of steaming noodles with a little pile of seafood on top.

Engella felt a pang of hunger – it was definitely time for her to eat. She checked her pockets and pulled out a single credit. She'd need to find more, but this was enough for now.

The server-bot who'd finished serving Engella's neighbour noticed she was there and accelerated towards her. It delivered her a glass of water and a menu while still managing to chop vegetables on the opposite side of the bar.

A little red light flashed on the side of the bot's head and its single camera-eye zoomed in and out, before it finally focussed on Engella's face.

'Good afternoon,' said Engella.

The server-bot made a whirring sound as its audio-system locked onto Engella's speech pattern. The computer whizzed and buzzed as it identified the appropriate language to converse in.

'Good morning, how can I be of service to you today?' the server-bot asked in a squeaky voice, which made Engella giggle.

'I'll have what he had,' Engella said, as she pointed at her neighbour's empty plate.

The bot bleeped in acknowledgement. 'Coming right up,' it said, as it zipped towards the kitchen. It grabbed a fresh pan and used its multiple arms to collect a pile of ingredients all stacked on top of each other: a cube of noodles, some vegetables, and some juicy-looking prawns. The stack wobbled, but the server-bot was incredibly skilled and managed to stop it from toppling over. The bot turned on the stove and then tossed the ingredients into a wok.

Engella gasped in wonder at the acrobatics of her lunch. The talented gymnast then switched its arms around, so that it was able to make use of one of its other utensils. It proceeded to scoop up a portion of chopped chilli and then sprinkled it into the wok, each and every piece landing perfectly on top of the neatly arranged vegetables.

The bot flipped the plate towards Engella, and it landed right on top of her place mat. A metal arm popped out of nowhere, handing her a pair of chopsticks and a spoon.

'Bravo!' Engella said, cheering and clapping her hands. She found herself with a wide grin, almost forgetting she had an important mission ahead of her. She ate her food quickly, now fully aware that she'd now been a resident in New Shanghai for several hours. The events of the holo-platform were still fresh in her mind. She needed to stay alert.

Back to work, she thought, as she gobbled the last piece of chilli prawn from her plate.

She suddenly felt uneasy but she didn't know why. She scanned the area, examining each of the other customers and looking out for anything unusual. Most of the other customers continued to eat their food, completely unaware of Engella watching them.

Except for one.

A man sat at a table on the opposite side of the plaza. He was wearing a scarf over his face and a baseball cap, so she couldn't make out his features. All she could see was his dark brown eyes looking back at her.

Their eyes met, and he looked away suddenly, after he'd realised that Engella had seen him looking.

α β γ

The man pretended to finish his food, then got up out of his seat.

And then he did something strange.

It looked as though he was talking to himself, but Engella soon realised that he was whispering into his lapel.

She jumped up from her seat, and suddenly felt claustrophobic, like the walls were closing in on her. She glanced back to check the man's position, but he had already disappeared into the crowds.

Engella turned around in a panic, not sure which way to go. She looked out for the best escape route but she could now see police drones located at every corner.

Had the man just given away her position? He could have been a spy working for the Hunters.

Not that it mattered anymore.

She had to make a run for it.

It wasn't long before she'd identified what appeared to be a secure escape route: a passageway on the opposite side of the plaza. She didn't wait for anything more to happen and had already sprinted off into the crowd when the server-bot yelled after her. 'Excuse me, madam!' it said, as it flailed its arms towards her. 'You haven't paid for your food!'

Engella ran into the crowds, and the server-bot gave up trying, bleeping out an emergency response code and instantly alerting the nearest police drone.

A drone which had hovered silently above the west corner of the plaza suddenly boomed into action, its sirens whining and its single bulb flashing blue. The drone moved slowly at first, scanning the faces of the people in the crowd until it was directly above Engella. She pulled the cloak of her hood up over her head and marched forwards, careful not to run in case it alerted the drone.

She looked around, panicked, but she could no longer see the man anywhere. She finally reached the passageway and then ran as fast as she could, not stopping until her lungs hurt.

This is bad ... really bad.

Engella didn't stand a chance against the Hunters and the city's police security systems. She rushed into another street, not looking where she was going, and crashed into a group of people who were standing in front of a food stall.

A furious man who had dropped his hotdog, covering his white shirt in ketchup and mustard, shouted several expletives towards Engella in a language which she'd never heard before. Thankfully for her she didn't understand what he had said, otherwise she would have been quite offended.

A woman, who had fallen backwards over several binbags of refuse dropped her purse, pouring out hundreds of credit chips into the street. Engella reached down and crawled along the floor to try and help the woman retrieve as many as possible while managing to pocket a handful in the process.

'I'm so sorry,' Engella said, as she placed a few credits into the woman's hand. 'I don't know what got into me!'

'Be more careful!' the woman yelled.

Engella could hear the sirens approaching. There was only one way to get out of this mess. She had enough problems with the Hunters always on her tail and couldn't deal with the police as well.

I need to lose the drone.

There was only one option, so she retraced her steps through the streets until she'd arrived back at the plaza. She looked out for the spy again, but she couldn't see him – or anyone else of concern, for that matter – so she returned to the place where she had been sitting, and found her plate of partially eaten noodles still sat there, now all cold and slimy.

'Sorry about that,' Engella said. 'My memory is terrible!' She reached out to the server-bot and dropped a credit chip into his hand.

'Thank you for your payment,' said the server-bot. The system bleeped a command, and the police drone returned to its original position, its light blinking out as it fell back into a state of semi-hibernation.

Engella took one last look out for the man, but he was nowhere to be seen. Her neck prickled. Had he alerted the Hunters? And were they about to attack?

She was terrified to think about what could happen next.

All she could do now was get as far away from the plaza as she possibly could.

2021-APR-17 14:44
COMPOUND, OUTSIDE TRUTH OR CONSEQUENCES, NEW MEXICO, UNITED STATES OF AMERICA

Annys had been alone in the dark for quite a long time, when there was suddenly a tap on the cell door. She listened carefully and prepared herself for yet another interrogation. She hoped it would be Lera again, who was much more forgiving than Tala.

The keycard system activated and the door unlocked with a clunk.

A guard entered with a bowl of porridge and a glass of water on a tray.

Annys sighed at the thought of yet another taste-less meal. 'What have you got for me today then, dear? Caviar or lobster? Or all of the above?'

Although most of the guard's face was concealed by

his helmet and visor, Annys saw him smile and give a brief nod, before he placed the tray down on the floor. He didn't say a word, yet Annys felt comfortable with him and she didn't quite understand why. She'd only been in prison for a short time, but it had been enough for them to build up some kind of rapport.

She found herself perplexed by his compassion towards her. He worked for the Hunters, after all. They hadn't even spoken, their connection had all been via small gestures: a smile here, or a laugh there.

Most of the other guards enjoyed all aspects of their role: including the opportunity to abuse the inmates.

But this man was different. He had been kind to her and, more importantly, he'd found her jokes funny – much to the disgust of his superiors. The last time Tala had caught him chuckling under his breath she'd almost hit him over the head with the butt of her blaster.

'Oh no,' said the guard, much to Annys's surprise. This had been the first time he'd spoken to her, after all. 'Far better than caviar.' He gestured towards the tray. 'Now eat up. You have a busy day ahead of you.'

Annys had no idea what the man was talking about, yet she was intrigued. She nodded, thanked him and walked over to the tray.

The guard closed the door behind him; the echo of the locking mechanism reverberating around the chamber.

Annys picked up the bowl of porridge and placed the spoon inside. She could feel something at the bottom. She placed her fingers into the gunk, and moved them around, until her eyes lit up with surprise.

She gasped, and pulled out a keycard.

Annys didn't know how or why the guard had helped her. But she could be sure about one thing.

She was getting out of prison that day.

β γ ᛐ

2066-OCT-24 14:34

NEW SHANGHAI CITY, ASIAN PROTECTORATE

Engella found a quiet park bench inside one of the recreational levels of the city's dome. GenMod birds fluttered about the glass ceiling above and the trees rustled in the artificially generated winds. She made notes in her journal, ensuring she wrote down every detail of the events of the last few days however insignificant they may have seemed. She had learned over the years that anything was possible with space-time travel, so it was important to record as many details as possible – she'd never know when they could save her life. She reviewed the data on her shiftband and noted each of the timepoints alongside the events which had occurred. She also added questions alongside her notes, like: who had helped her when she was attacked by the fleet of drones?

Next, Engella checked the map, which had been sketched out across two pages of her journal. She was now in the correct district, and wasn't far away from the location which the holocube had directed her to. Once she was as prepared as she was going to be, she left the bench and walked as casually as possible, but still made sure to avoid the high-definition cameras which lined the city's streets.

Some moments of the journey were more challenging than others, like when she had to cross the busy streets. All she could do was pull up her hood and keep her face down, while she traversed her way through the people, traffic and robots which passed by. Still, there was always a chance that her face would trigger some kind of system – but this was a risk she knew she needed to take.

Facial recognition was the cornerstone of late 21st century technology. It was used by every company, agency and corporation, and individuals too: who'd keep track of all aspects of their lives, from bank balances through to their personal music choices. Every aspect was activated and monitored by the shape of a person's face. This made it particularly challenging to move around the city of New Shanghai without detection.

Yet she had already planned that she'd leave as soon as she'd recovered the shiftbands. She just hoped that she'd be able to find them soon.

As she turned the pages of her journal, she came across the entries she'd written about Patrick. It was clear to her now that Annys had wanted Engella to meet him. And then there was the fact that Patrick had given her an important clue as to why her parents were on the run.

She was intrigued, and she wanted to know more about him. But, for now, she had to focus on the task at hand. Once she had the shiftbands safely in her possession, she'd return to Skye to meet Patrick again and take it from there. He probably didn't have all of the answers, but he was her only option right now. She'd need his support to rescue Annys, anyway. She just hoped he'd be willing to help her.

Engella entered a square which was surrounded by large cargo containers, their corrugated doors painted with their own unique logos – indicating which company they belonged to. On closer inspection, Engella realised many of the containers were not only used for storage, but they were in fact small offices filled with the hubbub of busy workers. Some of the containers had windows which had been cut out of the steel, and Engella could just about make out people working inside.

The middle of the square was busy with commuters, many of them in bright-eye-catching city-wear. New Shanghai City was renowned for its unique blend of fashion and art, and the show on that day was as vivid as any other. The square had a neat row of shrubs and a small water feature which ran around half of its perimeter. People sat on benches where they ate their lunch, worked, or chatted to their friends via hologram projection. Refuse-bots trundled along on their caterpillar tracks, as they removed discarded rubbish from the shrubs. At one point, a woman let out a little scream when a refuse-bot tried to clean away her shoes, which – unfortunately for her – she still happened to be wearing.

Engella looked at the bubbling water feature and the line of shrubs. There was something familiar about this place, and she wondered if she'd been there before. The streets of New Shanghai City all had a familiar feel, as the designs of each level were quite similar. Then again, as a young girl, she'd travelled around many of the city's districts so she'd covered a lot of ground. Perhaps, she had been there after all.

Engella approached a street sign and asked for directions to the business district. The sign, like all of the others she'd spoken to, was incredibly helpful, and told her the shortest route possible. She turned a corner and looked at the street name.

Evergreen Gardens. I've found it.

She'd arrived outside the front foyer of a sky-scraper, and looked up at a large screen which covered the first three floors. It flickered between several images, from a lake with crystal clear waters to the video of a man advertising some brand of washing powder. Eventually, it flicked back to the name of the company that resided there.

The letters glowed bright amber, and were so large they filled the entire screen...

GRAVITON DYNAMICS
Where the past and future unite

The words unsettled Engella, and she felt a shiver of anxiety. She'd found the location of her parents' research laboratory, and if that wasn't surprising enough, she'd discovered that the facility hadn't been deleted from the timeline yet. There was something about this place – this area in particular – that didn't seem quite right. All evidence elsewhere, with any link to her parents had been deleted – yet this remained.

I'm close. I can feel it.

She wondered when her parents had been there. Had it been years? Or perhaps only days? Her heart ached as she thought of her parents and what they must have gone through – the fear they had felt once they'd known the Hunters were after them. This wasn't helping, it only made her upset, so she tried to put it out of her mind.

She needed to continue her mission. She thought about her situation and there was something that didn't add up. She'd reached the place where the remaining shiftbands were supposed to be stored. Yet, why would her mother hide the shiftbands so close to her old research laboratory? Surely the Hunters would have searched every inch of this place by now.

Unless they'd missed something.

'Looking for anywhere in particular?' a gravelly voice said, from somewhere in the street behind her. Engella turned to find a man dressed in a dirty jump-suit emerging from the shadows. He had long blond matted hair which looked like it hadn't been washed for months. He leant against the wall, and looked

Engella up and down, through his narrowed eyes.

'No, I'm not looking for anywhere, thanks,' Engella said, as she moved her journal out of the man's sight.

'What have you got there?' he said, as he edged closer. 'Looks important.'

Engella knew there was no point in denying it – he'd clearly already seen her holding something. 'What this?' she asked. 'Oh, it's nothing. It's just my diary.' She now felt uneasy, so began to back away.

'Where are you going? We haven't finished talking yet,' the man said, as he smiled a sly smile; showing off his black rotten teeth.

'I'm going now,' Engella said, as she turned away. The events of the next few seconds happened so very fast that Engella hadn't realised they had happened at all.

Until it was too late.

The man had grabbed Engella's journal right out of her hands, and he had already sprinted halfway along the alleyway before Engella had chance to pursue him.

'No!' she yelled, as she chased after him, crashing into several people and a server-bot along the way. 'That man!' she yelled. 'He stole my journal!' Yet, no one even batted an eyelid.

She carried on with her pursuit, and was finally

able to catch up with him, after he had been blocked by a large group of tourists who filled most of the street.

Engella rugby-tackled the man, which sent him crashing to the ground. She snatched the journal from his hand and checked to make sure all of the pages were still there. The man got up and turned around to smile; showing his rotting teeth again. 'Almost had it,' he snapped, before he ran off.

By this point, the incident had generated so much of a buzz in the street, that people had started to gather around. Engella knew she had to avoid attention at all costs, so she decided it was best to back away. She ducked into a side street and was taken aback by the bright glare of a shop, halfway down the road.

The shop's neon sign placed above the door flashed brightly: CLONEPETZ.

Engella gazed into the window to see animals of all shapes and sizes – literally. There were two large glass window displays on either side of the shop, so the public who passed by could view the animals – probably so they'd be so infatuated they'd have to go inside and buy one. On one side, a tiny Indian elephant rolled around in a bowl of water, while a black and white tiger the size of a tabby cat played with a ball of string on the other.

The door creaked open to reveal an elderly woman dressed in a flowered gown standing at the counter. She was stroking a large cockatoo with a multitude of coloured feathers, who squawked at Engella as she approached the counter.

'Welcome to CLONEPETZ!' the woman said. 'How can I help you today?'

'Hello,' said Engella. 'How much is it to get myself a replication pack?'

'That would be eight credits.'

Engella counted the remaining credits she had in her pocket to find that she didn't have enough. She sighed. 'Ah, okay ... I only have five.'

'What were you looking for today?'

'I was going to get a present, for a friend of mine.'

'Well, I'm in a good mood today, and because you're such a sweet young girl, I'll let you have one for five credits. But I only have this one left.' She held out a replication pack that looked like a bag of ooze with a bluey-white tinge. It had a slight glow to it, too. 'Hope you don't mind a few squid genes spliced in, do you?'

'Thank you, I really appreciate it,' Engella said. 'Yes, the squid genes are fine. I think...'

Engella paid, and the lady passed her the replication pack.

'What do I do with it?'

'Oh, you're a CLONEPETZ newbie! How exciting. You just need to take some DNA from the animal of your choice – best to use a cutting of hair if you can get it – and put it inside the top of the pack. Once you're ready to go, just activate it and leave it somewhere warm. Not too hot though.'

'Okay, sounds easy enough.'

Engella thanked the woman and left the shop. Once she'd returned to the street, she wasn't exactly sure which way to go. She looked across the road to get her bearings.

And there it was.

A lion's head, made from black marble.

The Cowardly Lion from *The Wizard of Oz*. Right there, in plain sight.

Engella had never understood why the Cowardly Lion in her holocube movie had been shaded to black. But it was finally as clear as day. Patrick had explained how Engella's parents said they'd stored the remaining shiftbands in a storage facility.

Lion Storage. I've found it.

The holocube was a message, after all, and the Cowardly Lion a clue to finding the right place.

Engella concealed herself as much as possible, then

staked out the building from afar. It was clear the facility had strict security protocols: plenty of facial recognition technology to scan her face and biometric scanners to process her DNA. It would be a challenge to get inside. She observed multiple security droids as they marched around the gates of the building.

This is impossible. She had no idea how she'd make it inside.

And then, she saw him – the man from the plaza – watching her from the opposite side of the road. Engella's first instinct was to run, but the man didn't look like a threat. It was as if he wanted her to see him. He still wore his cap low over his brow, with his face mostly covered by his scarf. He clearly didn't want to be identified.

Engella noticed that he held something in his hand. In fact, he seemed to be waving it towards her.

Impossible. It can't be.

It was Engella's journal.

She could make out the turquoise-patterned cover, and the brown leather strap which held the pages together. She felt a wave of panic, terrified at the prospect that the street-thief who had stolen her journal, had replaced it with a fake. She reached inside her rucksack anxiously and was surprised to discover her journal was exactly where she'd left it.

She removed it carefully, and flicked through the pages, and was relieved to discover it was definitely the original.

The man waited to get Engella's attention and then pointed towards the building beside the storage facility. She looked up to see a narrow electronic message board, which had been built into the panelling above the second floor. It was basic in its design, with just enough memory to store simple messages – news alerts, weather reports and the like – which moved along the screen until they reached the end, when another would take its place.

The man held a portable computer with a small satellite dish attached by a cable. He tapped on the keyboard, keeping one eye on the screen while looking towards the electronic message board at the same time. Engella followed his line of sight until her eyes met the message board, and watched as the most recent news bulletin was replaced by a simple message:

I'VE GOT YOUR BACK

Engella looked at the man and nodded in understanding. She watched as he continued to type at his laptop, and then gestured towards the foyer of the building. He threw something towards the door and Engella watched as it tumbled across the ground, stopping just outside the entrance. Engella looked at him, unsure what to do, and he gestured toward the message board again.

TAKE IT

The message quickly faded and was replaced by another:

WHEN I GIVE THE WORD – GO INSIDE

He held up his hand and used his fingers as a countdown. Three. Two. One. And then, a final message appeared on screen:

GO. NOW!

Engella's gaze returned towards *Lion Storage* to see the lights on every single floor go out in a flash – the building now plunged into complete darkness.

The building's power had been temporarily interrupted, so she finally had her chance. With the power down, the security systems had all gone offline and they wouldn't go back on until the backup generators kicked in.

Engella didn't give it another thought, and had already made her way towards the foyer. She ducked down to the ground and picked up the small device which had been tossed there by the unidentified man.

The building's emergency alarms began to chime as the drain in power switched them on automatically. The people inside began to evacuate each floor; office workers, maintenance staff and visitors all flooding into the street.

Engella fought against the tide of people and made her way past the staircases and slipped into the service elevator. She waited until the last person had left, before making her way up the stairs.

The emergency alarm continued to ring, and Engella had no idea which way to go. A few stragglers appeared on the stairs, so Engella turned towards the wall and tried to cover her face.

'Hey, you! We need to evacuate!' a man shouted.

Engella pretended not to hear and ran the other way. She reached the landing of the first floor but had no idea which way to go next. A noise startled her, and she realised it was coming from her pocket. She removed the smartphone which had been thrown to her by the unidentified man.

The smartphone rang loudly, so she answered it.

'Take the service stairwell,' the man said, in a strong American accent. 'There won't be anyone there. The shiftbands are stored in Archive 17. You'll know which box. I'm sorry I can't help you any further, but somebody else needs my help right now. I have to go.'

'Thank you,' Engella said. 'Who are you?'

'All at the right time, Engella. All at the right time,' he said, and promptly hung up.

Engella followed the route to Archive 17, just like the man had told her. She removed the sheet of paper which Patrick had given to her before she left and tapped the code into the keypad. The locking mechanism buzzed, and turned a bright green, the lock opening up with a clank.

Engella entered the unit and passed by a number of rolling stacks. She quickly established the layout, made her way to the correct shelf and found Patrick's safety deposit box exactly where he said it would be. She typed in the additional key code he'd given her – a number now etched in her mind – she had memorised it digit by digit, after all – and waited for the box to open. The box beeped and the red light outside turned to a vibrant green.

She sighed, anxious to get inside, and waited for the hatch to open.

Inside, there was a pile of research notes resting on top of a decorated box. Engella bundled the files into her rucksack and lifted the box's lid. It was full to the brim with a dark green foam with five impressions inside, four of them containing a shiftband.

She gasped as she saw them for the first time.

Each one was labelled with a different Greek letter, as she'd expected - she'd recognised them instantly as they looked exactly like the symbols which had been etched into the bottom of the holocube she'd discovered all those years before.

$$\alpha - \beta - \gamma - \delta - \varepsilon$$

She read them aloud... Alpha, Beta, Gamma, Delta, and Epsilon.

The impression labelled with Alpha was empty, yet Beta, Delta, Gamma and Epsilon were safely tucked away inside. Engella checked her own shiftband against the ones in the box, and noted she was wearing Beta. Her Beta – the one in her timepoint – was scratched and aged, whereas the Beta shiftband in the box was shiny and new. Each shiftband had its own distinct colour, in addition to its own symbol. Engella looked at her shiftband and noted the yellow β etched into its side.

I've found them. I actually did it!

She replaced the lid, and it clicked shut, sending an echo through the room.

Something rattled from inside the facility.

Then, another sound, this time like a large object as it was scraped across the metal floor.

Engella held her breath and listened intently. There was something else inside. And it was getting closer.

She packed the box inside her rucksack, closed the archive unit as she had found it, and left the room. She checked the corridors before she entered them but there was no one there. She breathed a sigh of relief. Perhaps she had been hearing things. She was on edge, after all. Perhaps the sound of the doors closing shut had activated some type of internal security system.

Engella relaxed a little and walked into the main floor area of the archive to find a tall security-bot stood in front of her. She yelped as it bounded towards her, its arms flailing.

She tried to pull away but it had grabbed her wrist. She pushed back and they both tumbled to the floor. She managed to break free of the robot's grasp and sprinted down the corridor, slamming the door behind her.

Engella bolted down the stairs and through a side exit, joining the crowds who were milling around outside. The alarms had subsided and the security systems had now been reactivated. She'd made it out just in time.

She wandered through the streets until she was a few blocks away, then finally ducked into a side street full of refuse containers. Out of view, this was the perfect place to shift away. Fully aware she could be tracked back to Skye, Engella planned to activate a multi-shift, just like she'd always used. After all, she didn't want anyone following her back to the cottage.

She looked at the walls and noticed they were plastered with old posters. One had an advertisement for a brand of dog food and Engella smiled at the photograph which showed a Cairn Terrier. It looked exactly like Toto – Dorothy's pet dog from *The Wizard of Oz*.

She had a moment of familiarity; a flash of recognition.

There was rustling among the shadows, and Engella could make out a person hidden there.

She reached inside her backpack and pulled out the holocubes. She made sure that she had the correct one and placed the others back inside. Using a penknife from her utility belt, she began to scratch a message into the holocube's base.

She signed it using her initials – ER, like her papa always did.

She placed the holocube on the ground, and activated it, leaving it to play.

The lights flickered across the alleyway.

She pulled back her sleeve. 'Shift,' she said. A portal materialised, and she disappeared inside.

The little girl, who had been searching for food among the refuse containers, stepped out, and watched the lights in awe.

ₐ β γ

βΩ

MULTI-SHIFT: SPACE-TIME COORDINATES DELETED

Engella travelled through several times and places, to ensure her trail through space-time was erratic and difficult to track. First of all she'd found herself in a baking desert, which she discovered was an unmapped area of the North African Sahara. Sand dunes went on for miles and the ferocious sun shone down, as hot as a burning furnace.

The heat was excruciating and sweat poured from Engella's brow. After walking for a mile or so, she gulped down the last drops from her water bottle. She'd need to find a water source, and she'd need to find one soon. The temperature was too high; the conditions too extreme. Still, she'd left a trail of quarks there, which meant that any Hunters on her tail would also have to walk the same treacherous path that she'd followed.

As she shifted away, she was relieved to find herself in a much more comfortable environment. This time, she'd travelled halfway across the globe, and had landed in a temperate rainforest in New Zealand. The dry air of the desert had been replaced by the breeze of a bustling jungle. The damp air soothed Engella's parched throat.

She meandered along a trail, pushing though twisted branches which were covered in a veil of bright green moss. She gazed at the arching fronds of the tree ferns on all sides. She eventually heard the trickle of a stream and rushed over to the water's edge, splashing her face and using her hands to drink. She filled up her bottle before continuing along the trail. The slopes of the hillside suddenly steepened, and it was quite exhausting to make it through the foliage, but she pushed onwards. The more difficult the journey was for her, the more difficult it would be for any Hunters in pursuit. The chatter from deep within the rainforest was deafening as she travelled higher into the canopy. She traversed a rockface which was elevated almost twenty metres above the jungle below. Once she'd reached its peak, she decided it was a good time to shift again.

'Enjoy the climb,' she said, smiling, as she thought about the unsuspecting Hunters who would attempt to follow her.

βζ φ

Engella emerged from the brightness of the portal to find herself in darkness. She'd planned for one last shift before she returned to the Isle of Skye, and had decided upon Central London in the near past; a place where it would be easy to get lost in the crowds. She rummaged inside her rucksack and retrieved her flashlight. She had expected to arrive in the bustling city streets, but it was obvious she'd taken a wrong turn in space-time.

The air was warm and humid, and beads of sweat formed on her brow. She could taste something metallic in the air. Exhaust fumes, perhaps.

Suddenly there was a rumble from somewhere in

the distance, and warm winds began to tumble around.

The sound intensified. Something was approaching, and it was moving fast.

This isn't good.

The rumble was now a roar, and Engella realised where she had materialised.

She flashed her torch, illuminating the path ahead.

The tracks reflected the light from the torch. She was in a train tunnel.

'Nope ... not good at all,' she said, as she looked each way in a panic. At first, she wasn't sure which way the train was coming from, but it wasn't long before she found out. She watched in terror as two bright headlights rushed at her from out of nowhere, like the eyes of a demon stirring from its slumber.

Run!

The train rattled towards her, and it quickly dawned on her that she'd never be able to outrun it, so she prepared to shift instead.

The rumble was replaced by a mild shudder, and the train eventually slowed to a complete stop. Engella glanced along the track to try and work out why the train hadn't run her over yet, and she noticed a set of traffic lights suspended from the side of the tunnel wall, one light shining a deep red.

Today's my lucky day.

The train was on hold. She still had time to run, so she used her torch to light the track ahead. She wasn't sure if the tracks were electrified, so she made sure not to touch them, running along the sides instead.

She heard the rumble as the train began to move again. She didn't think she'd make it – but as she reached for her shiftband, something caught her eye.

'A light at the end of the tunnel!' she yelled. 'Today, *is* my lucky day!'

It was the next station, and it was only a short sprint away. She could make it, as long as she ran as fast as she could. She ran, not looking behind her, before finally bursting out from the tunnel into the brightness of the station.

People who were waiting for the train to arrive gasped as they watched Engella emerge from the mouth of the tunnel. Their surprise was quickly replaced by screams and shouts, as panic spread among the crowds.

'Help!' Engella said, 'Help me up!'

Engella turned back to see the lights of the train rumbling into view. By now she could make out the light from the cabin, the train driver's eyes wide as she realised there was a girl on the tracks. The train screeched as the driver slammed on the brakes.

'Give me your hand,' a young woman yelled.

Engella clambered forwards, reaching out her hands, and the woman bent down and grabbed her wrist.

The woman pulled with everything she had, and they both tumbled backwards onto the platform.

Engella lay beside the woman, breathing heavily, still a little stunned. She could see the logo of the *London Underground* on the wall.

Aha. That's where I am.

The space-time coordinates had been right after all, she'd just ended up a lot deeper than she'd expected. She lifted herself up and realised she was covered from head to toe in soot.

People were staring back at her in silence, their expressions filled with shock, surprise, or something in between.

'Help is on its way,' a man said from somewhere within the crowd. He'd called the emergency services using one of the phones on the platform.

'No!' Engella yelled. 'I need to get out of here. But thanks anyway!' She nodded at the woman who had helped her, and pushed her way through the crowd.

'Wait!' the woman said, but Engella had already left through an exit.

Once she was sure she'd found a quiet spot, she prepared to shift away. She couldn't wait to return to the cottage.

Her journey had been a little more eventful than she had hoped, and she'd had far too much excitement for one day.

Engella returned to the beach at Rubha Shlèite and followed her usual route to the cottage. After checking the coordinates, she noted that it had been several hours since she'd left.

Patrick gasped as Engella entered the cottage, her clothes covered with soot. 'Christ! 'What happened to you?' he asked, as he grabbed a towel from the kitchen. 'Here, take this.'

'Where do you want me to start?' Engella replied. She tapped her shiftband, and a holographic display appeared between them. She waved her hand and scrolled through the data, until she'd found what she was looking for. 'Okay, here goes … I left here around ten hours ago.'

'Ten hours?!' Patrick said, surprised. 'Engella, it's only been a few minutes since you left...' He paused and placed his hand on his chin. 'When I first met you, I was really confused. I didn't understand how it was possible. You're so much older than ... well ...' He held back from saying something. 'It just didn't make any sense to me.'

'Older? What do you mean?'

'Engella, listen. This is not going to be easy. The research – what your parents and I were working on – let's just say, it was groundbreaking ... so we didn't quite know how space-time travel would work. I believed we were in control, but since meeting you, and seeing the technology in use, I've realised something important. I've made a big discovery.'

Engella sat down and waited for Patrick to continue. 'Go on,' she said.

'It's obvious to me now. It blows our original theories out of the water. I told you it's been five years since I saw your parents ...'

'Yes?'

'The last time I saw them was when we escaped from the research lab.' Patrick paused. 'The Company was onto us. They knew we were going to take our research and run. We didn't agree with the direction they were taking us in. The tech was supposed to help people, but all they could see were dollar signs. Your mother had already secured the shiftbands by this point.'

'I found them,' Engella said, as she reached inside her rucksack. 'They were exactly where the holocubes said they'd be.' She pulled out the box and placed it on the sitting room table.

Patrick opened it up and looked inside. 'It's been a while,' he said. 'There was one thing left for us to do. Our computer system was full to the brim with data, all our research spanning several years. I made as many notes by hand as possible. I spent hours copying it out, before we were ready to delete the servers. We were almost finished when the Hunters attacked. I was with your parents and you were there too.'

'I found your files,' Engella said, as she passed the pile of research papers to Patrick.

'Oh, how wonderful, thank you so much.' Patrick placed the files beside him and looked Engella in the eyes. 'What do you remember about the day we were all separated?' he asked. 'Do you remember anything?'

'I don't remember anything, no.'

Patrick nodded. 'You were only babies at the time. I didn't expect you would.'

'The first memory I have is of my parents on the beach. The three of us. We'd often move around from place to place, but it was only when I was older that I understood why. We were on the run.'

'Yes, I thought as much. You were both so very young. You were only one and a half when you were separated. I have something to tell you, and it's not going to make sense to start with. Your mother prepared to shift, and the wormhole opened, but the Company came in by force. Two of us made it through, but the portal collapsed before you and your parents could follow. We were separated. You were with your mother and father while Annika was with me. I was holding her as I made it through the portal.'

'Annika?'

A car horn beeped from outside, and Engella could hear the crunch of stones as a vehicle turned into the drive.

'Is it that time already?' Patrick said. 'Ah yes, school's finished. They're here.'

Engella sat patiently and waited for Patrick to continue.

'Engella, go and sit up on the hillside,' Patrick said. 'Annika loves it up there. We'll join you soon.'

'Who are you talking about?' Engella said, as her

eyes welled up. Yet, deep down in her heart, she knew.

Patrick placed his hand on her shoulder. 'Don't worry. It's going to be okay. We'll see you there. There's someone important I need you to meet.'

๑   ๑   ๑

Engella reached the hillside, as the setting sun turned the sky from orange to pink. The place was perfectly peaceful, except for the occasional chorus of bird song. She relaxed, then she heard voices, and an infectious laugh which made her smile.

Her heart throbbed. She could hear Patrick talking now, telling jokes which made the other person giggle.

Engella could make them both out now; Patrick on one side and a young girl on the other. For a moment they blocked out the setting sun and Engella had to squint, trying to see them through the glare. She thought back: the toys inside the cupboard, the child's bedroom. She'd wondered who they belonged to but she'd never considered this.

The young girl skipped and laughed, as she tugged on Patrick's hand, urging him to walk faster. 'Come on, Patrick, let's race!' the little girl said, her accent so very familiar.

Engella looked into the girl's eyes and memories

of her own childhood flashed before her. The sense of familiarity was overwhelming.

'I don't understand,' said Engella. 'How is this possible?'

'I'd like to introduce you to someone,' said Patrick. The girl looked into Engella's eyes and hid behind Patrick's leg. She peered around and pulled back again and hid once she'd noticed Engella was looking.

'You're not shy, are you?' asked Patrick. 'Why don't you say hello? This is someone very special. Don't be scared.'

The girl peered around Patrick's leg, and smiled – before returning to her safe place again.

'Hello, my name's Engella. What's yours?'

'I planned to change her name when we arrived,' Patrick whispered, out of ear shot of the little girl. 'For protection of course. This is your twin sister, Engella. Annika Rhys.'

Engella lowered herself and reached out her arms. The little girl looked up at Patrick and inched her way forwards. Engella couldn't believe the resemblance. They were identical, in the sense that the little girl looked exactly like Engella had done at that age.

'Annika, darling. This is your sister. She's been travelling for a long time, but you were both born on the same day,' Patrick said.

'Hello, Annika ...' Engella said, as she tried to hold back the tears. 'It's so very nice to meet you.'

Annika smiled, and ran into Engella's arms, and Engella couldn't hold it back any longer. She burst into tears and held the child close.

'Why are you sad?' Annika asked.

'Oh, I'm not sad, Annika. These are happy tears. I'm very, very happy to meet you.'

Annika accepted this and didn't appear to be affected by it either, as she jumped away, her face full of excitement. 'Do you like to play games?' she asked.

'Oh yes ... I definitely do. What game shall we play?'

Patrick stepped away and placed his arms behind his back. He smiled as he watched the reunion with glee, nodding at Engella. 'How about I go back to the cottage and prepare some dinner? You can play with Engella and get to know each other while I'm gone, okay?'

'Yes, Grandpa,' Annika said.

'Grandpa?' Engella said.

Patrick smiled. 'In name only,' he said. 'I'll tell you everything, I promise.'

Engella understood and watched him leave as he allowed the reunited sisters to spend some quality time together.

'What game shall we play, then?'

'Do you like flowers?'

'I love flowers,' Engella said, as she still tried to take it all in. 'Have you ever made a daisy chain before?'

Annika shook her head. 'What's that?' she asked.

'You've never made a daisy chain before? Well, have I got something wonderful to show you.'

They played together on the grass. Engella picked daisies from the bank, tied their stalks together and formed a chain of flowers.

She placed it around Annika's wrist and tied the last of the stalks together. Annika gasped with pure delight at this and gazed lovingly into her sister's eyes. 'I like having a sister,' she said.

'I do too,' Engella said, as she placed her arm around Annika's shoulder. 'I haven't seen my family in a very long time. I'm so happy to spend time with you.' She managed to hold back the tears this time. But only just. Her world was now much more complicated than she'd ever imagined.

The urgency of Annys's rescue had become even more apparent. She had been so focused on the search for her parents, it hadn't occurred to her that what she was seeking had been right in front of her all along.

She'd finally found her family again. She had a sister. And she needed to rescue her.

'I know why I was sent here now,' Engella said. 'I need to save Annys.'

'I'm here silly,' Annika said.

'I thought your name was Annika?'

'I'm Annys too. That's my other name.'

Engella picked up Annika's hand, and held it tightly, 'I won't let you down,' she said. 'I promise. But I need to go soon.'

'Won't you stay a while longer?' Annika asked. 'We can make more daisy chains!'

'I'm sorry. We'll see each other again … I'm not sure exactly when it'll be, but we'll definitely see each other again, I promise.'

🔍 🔍 🔍

Later, Engella led Annika back to the cottage to meet Patrick who was gardening outside. He had taken a small cutting from a bushy oregano plant beneath the windowsill, which was buzzing with bees and butterflies. Engella could see a kind-faced woman through the window, who looked up briefly and gave Engella a wave.

Patrick ducked around the door, and spoke to the

woman inside. It looked as though she'd been preparing a meal for them all. 'Come out and meet Engella, darling,' he said.

The short woman came outside and removed her navy-blue pinafore, before folding it neatly and placing it on top of the wall. 'Oh, hello, dear,' she said. 'It's lovely to finally meet you.' She placed her hand in Patrick's and smiled at Engella, her face friendly and bright.

Engella smiled back as she realised that there was more to their relationship than she'd first realised.

'Nice to meet you too.'

'Annika stays with Mrs Macintosh while I work in town,' said Patrick. He lit his pipe, took a puff, and placed it on the windowsill. 'I don't know what's coming, Engella. I thought I did, but all of this has shown me there's no point in even guessing … Annika, darling, why don't you go upstairs and play? I need to talk to Engella about something important.'

'Okay, Grandpa,' said Annika, who skipped towards the door. She turned to face Engella. 'Will you come upstairs and look at my dolls soon, Engella?'

'Yes, of course I will. I'll be there soon.'

'I'll leave you both to catch up,' Mrs Macintosh said.

They thanked her and waited until they were alone.

'So why does she call you Grandpa?' Engella asked.

'That's what we tell people. It's easier that way. I can't really explain it otherwise, so I just pretend she's my granddaughter. None of us know what's coming, Engella. In fact, I'm sure you know more about my future than I do. You'll be needing these, though,' he said, as he placed the box of shiftbands on the wall surrounding the flowerbed.

Engella opened the box and reached inside. 'Why don't you take two?' she asked. 'One for Annika and one for you.'

'Oh no, I don't need one. I'll be staying here.' He gestured towards the window, where they could see Mrs Macintosh as she set up the table. 'I have a life here.'

Engella understood completely. 'Well, hold on to this one, then,' she said. 'Annika will need it, one day.' She handed Patrick the Beta shiftband from the box, which was all shiny and new.

'Annys needs you now,' said Patrick. 'Annika is safe here, with us.'

Engella nodded. 'I'm ready to go back now. I need to save her.'

'You know what you need to do, Engella. The Lights of Time, remember. You can follow them to the place where they've taken her. You just need to get close enough.'

Engella checked her shiftband's memory, and a hologram appeared. She reviewed data from all of the places she'd visited over the last few days, and eventually found the coordinates of the Yixing Forest.

'Move carefully, Engella. Find somewhere nearby, but not too close otherwise you'll be detected. Use the Hunters' own methods against them for a change. They won't know what hit them. Find Annys and get her to safety. She'll know what to do.'

Engella walked over to Patrick and hugged him close. 'Thank you for everything,' she said. 'It was wonderful to meet you. I feel like I know my parents a little better now, thanks to you. It means a lot.'

'You're welcome,' said Patrick. 'I'm just glad the little one has someone so courageous to watch over her. Watch her for me, okay?'

Engella smiled at Patrick. 'Watcher,' she said. 'I get it now.'

She was about to leave, when something suddenly occurred to her. 'Don't forget to turn the inhibitor on again,' she said. 'Annika can switch it off when she's ready.'

Patrick nodded. 'I'll tell her.'

Engella entered the coordinates of the Yixing Forest, and made sure she'd arrive around five minutes before she'd left Annys behind. A beam of light shone brightly from Engella's shiftband and Annika, who'd noticed the lights outside, ran down the stairs and out into the garden followed closely by Mrs Macintosh – their mouths wide open at the shock of it all.

The family watched in awe as a whirlpool of lights engulfed Engella.

'Bye!' Annika yelled.

Engella's heart ached at the thought of leaving. Yet, she was content in the knowledge that her sister was loved and cared for in this place, and more importantly – she was safe. It was Annys who needed her now.

'Here goes,' said Engella.

Patrick waved. 'Goodbye, my friend. And remember. There's never enough time. Use it wisely.'

Engella waved goodbye, and stepped into the vortex.

2066-OCT-23 21:50

YIXING FOREST, GREATER NEW SHANGHAI METROPOLIS

Engella hid behind a tree in the Yixing Forest as she listened to the shouts and whistles from deep within the shadows. Without using any light to guide her, she tiptoed her way along the trail. The forest appeared quite different shrouded in darkness, branches looming like a giant hand about to snatch her into the night. She could hear a commotion coming closer. It sounded as though someone was crashing their way through the undergrowth, with twigs and branches cracking under their weight.

She waited in silence and found a hiding place with a direct view of the trail ahead.

A person emerged from the trees: a girl – rushing

as fast as she could to get away from someone pursuing her.

It was a strange feeling to see her previous self in this way, like she was watching a home movie of her memories. But this wasn't a movie – it was her past. And this time around, she already knew the ending.

The other Engella – her past-self – needed her help.

She covered her mouth in shock as an explosion blasted only metres above the girl's head, startling her enough to stop her in her tracks. She looked both ways, terrified and unsure which way to go, before cowering behind a tree stump.

Engella waited for the Hunter to arrive and he was there exactly when she expected him to be. He slowed his pursuit, and flashed his torch around, illuminating his face briefly so Engella could see him head on. He had a snake tattoo which covered most of his neck, and he smiled wickedly while he taunted the frightened girl, like a fox about to pounce on its prey.

She tried to keep her emotions in check, but she couldn't hold it in anymore. The way in which he had taunted her – and how it gave him pleasure too – sent anger bubbling to the surface.

She dropped to her knees, and squelched her fingers through the mud, scraping through the under-growth until she felt something sharp graze her finger. She picked up the rock, and sprinted at the Hunter, approaching him from behind, and smashed it into the back of his head. She gasped when he let out a groan, grabbed his head and tumbled down the hillside; shocked at what she'd done. Yet, her guilt faded and turned to relief, as soon as she saw her past-self escape uninjured.

She followed her silently and watched as the events unfolded as she knew they would.

'There's no place like home,' her past-self said, before disappearing through a wormhole.

Engella hid silently and waited for the Hunters to activate their shiftbands. Using her V-Dis, she reviewed the stream of data which flooded in. Soon, the analysis was complete, and the Hunters' destination flashed up. She gasped at the realisation of where they'd gone, and where she needed to follow.

After waiting for the last Hunter to shift away, she entered the space-time coordinates. She'd been pursued by the Hunters' for far too long, and now it was her turn to pursue them. It felt good. She was now the Hunter, and they had become her prey.

It was about time they experienced a taste of their

own medicine, anyway. She removed her blaster from its holster.

The wormhole opened, and she stepped inside – her blaster pointed forwards defiantly, ready to shoot anyone who had the nerve to get in her way.

β γ ⊕

2021-APR-17 16:13

**COMPOUND, OUTSIDE TRUTH OR CONSEQUENCES,
NEW MEXICO, UNITED STATES OF AMERICA**

Engella gripped her binoculars and surveyed the scene below. She'd tracked the Hunters through space-time to their compound, and had returned to her vantage point on the hill beside Turtleback Mountain. She was surprised how much the compound had changed in the period since she and Annys had last been there. Before, it had been an unoccupied, almost abandoned, military base. Now though, it was considerably more. Convoys of armoured vehicles drove across the desert, while fleets of drones circled the skies like vultures. She read the signage which had been reinforced above the main gates, and it sent a shiver down her spine.

HUNTCORP

It looks like they've had an upgrade, she thought. *Better name, too.* 'The Huntington Corporation' was a bit of a tongue-twister, after all.

She tapped her V-Dis and reviewed the space-time coordinates, discovering that five years had passed since she'd last been there. She considered her options: she could approach the compound from the desert and try to traverse the wall, but that would almost certainly result in detection, so she decided upon the more viable option: travel into the town and look for a way to access the compound from there.

She walked into the desert for at least a kilometre, ensuring she was as far away from the compound's exclusion zone as possible, until she eventually reached the town of Truth or Consequences.

The town was desolate: buildings had been bulldozed, and those that remained had been boarded up. It was now a ghost town.

'Eddie,' Engella said sadly, thinking of the boy. 'What happened here?'

The rumble of a vehicle's engine from a side road made Engella jump, and she dipped behind a road sign. Silently she waited, and watched as a vehicle came to a stop just outside of what had remained of the old town square.

A guard in a HuntCorp uniform stepped out of the vehicle and leant on the door while he lit up a cigarette. He wore a black, fitted jumpsuit and a black helmet with a reflective visor. The driver of the vehicle joined him and they started talking, but they were too far away for Engella to hear what they were saying.

She scurried across the sandy road, her blaster pointed – ready to fire if necessary – and made her way to the back of the truck. She used the barrel of her blaster to lift the green tarpaulin which hung across the cargo hold. Once she was assured there were no more guards inside, she climbed in and covered herself in camouflage netting which had been piled up inside.

Engella waited nervously, relaxing a little once she heard the engine start up again. They set off along the highway before turning off into a sideroad. They'd clearly moved onto a desert track as the road was bumpy and uneven, shaking the vehicle from side to side. Engella struggled to hold on and at one point she almost toppled over, when the vehicle went over a hump.

After a turbulent twenty minutes the vehicle slowed, before finally screeching to a halt.

Engella listened carefully and could just about hear the guards as they were processed through security. They had arrived at the outer checkpoint, and after a brief conversation with the senior security guard, the vehicle was authorised to continue. Before long they were on the move again.

They accelerated down the long, winding road that ambled around the compound. They arrived at their destination, drawing to a stop, and the guards got out, slamming the doors behind them.

Engella peeked from behind the tarpaulin and watched the guards as they made their way to the nearest barracks. They'd parked in an open courtyard, and there was no way Engella would be able to climb out without being seen by someone – or something. She could hear the buzz of drones as they scanned the base below, and something else – like metal scraping across the ground. She tried to look out to see where it was coming from, but it was somewhere out of sight.

The tarpaulin was suddenly pulled back in one swoop to reveal a tall robot, waiting to scan the contents inside.

That didn't take long, Engella thought, as she cowered, expecting to be captured. But the machine just stared at her with its saucer-like eyes barely moving – like it had been frozen in space-time.

The machine began to ring, as if it had a smartphone trapped inside, but it wasn't long before Engella realised that the sound was coming from her own rucksack.

'Holy shh...!' she mumbled, as she scrambled to locate the device. After finding it in a fluster, she switched it to silent and turned on the vibrate function, before finally accepting the call.

'Hello?' she whispered.

'Hey kiddo, I'm just sorting out your ride ... should be ready in three ... two ... one... now.'

A hatch on the robot's underside swung open to reveal a compartment almost big enough to hide inside. Almost. It looked as though it would be a tight fit.

Kiddo? 'Who are you?' Engella asked.

'A good friend. You'll know soon enough. The delivery-bot will take you into the main compound, but you'll need to find your own way to the prison barracks. You'll find Annys there ... Shoot, someone's coming – got to go...' And with that, the man hung up.

Engella placed the smartphone in her top pocket and struggled to climb inside, but she had enough room if she sat with her legs close to her chest. She just about managed it, and closed the hatch behind her. She felt a swift movement as the robot began to travel, its caterpillar tracks rumbling across the courtyard. She was able to see through the gap in the hatch door, giving her the occasional glimpse of the outside world. Troops marched by; the stamp of their boots so loud it felt as though they were right on top of her.

The robot took a turn and joined a queue of similar-looking machines, which all appeared to be undertaking deliveries or completing other important tasks. The queue was slow and Engella began to sweat: the longer the journey took, the more chance she had of being detected.

As the delivery-bot approached the front of the queue, Engella realised that they were undergoing additional scans at the security gate.

She gulped at the prospect of sneaking through the scans undetected.

The machine finally reached the front of the line, and the guard stationed there used a barcode reader to check it off the system. The system bleeped, and the lights around the gate flashed from green to red.

'Hold it,' the senior guard said, furrowing his brow. He peered at the bot with contempt and checked the data on the security system. 'Something's not right.'

Engella held her breath and closed her eyes.

She was only metres away from the man, and she could just about see his expression through the gap in the door.

'This isn't supposed to be here!' he yelled, as he turned to another guard who was stationed outside the door. 'Sort it out, will you?'

'Yes, sir,' said the other guard, who rushed off somewhere out of view.

Engella watched as he returned holding a V-Dis. He proceeded to scan the identification chip of the machine, before turning to face his superior.

'It's okay, sir,' he said. 'Registration was filed in the wrong place. Food transfer. It's right here, look.' The man flashed the screen towards his superior, who seemed satisfied enough.

'Okay, let it through,' the senior guard said. They activated the door, and it slid open with a *whoosh*.

The machine moved inside and journeyed through a network of corridors.

Engella couldn't believe her luck. She honestly didn't think she'd make it so far without being detected – and had expected a fight much earlier.

The mysterious caller had done an excellent job of getting her inside.

The delivery-bot halted inside a short corridor and powered down. Engella assumed this was her stop, so she lifted the hatch and made sure she was alone, before climbing out.

The smartphone buzzed inside her pocket, and she was quick to answer.

'Okay … you're in,' the man said. 'Wait there until I tell you to get out.'

'Erm, okay …' Engella replied. 'What happens if I get out before you tell me to get out?'

The man didn't have chance to reply.

Red emergency lights flashed, and a siren whined so loudly that Engella had to cover her ears.

A voice boomed across the internal speakers. 'Unauthorised access. Section 0909-2108-0610,' it stated robotically.

'Uh-oh … I think I already know the answer …' Engella said, but the man had already hung up. He'd obviously given up on her by now, as she clearly didn't stand a chance.

Panicked, Engella readied her blaster, as it was inevitable she'd have company soon.

The doors at the end of the corridor slid open, and a squadron of guards in full HuntCorp riot gear marched inside.

There was nowhere to go, so Engella prepared to fight.

They were quick to open fire.

Engella ducked as bullets ricocheted off the wall – missing her head by inches and hitting a light fixture instead, which exploded, sending shrapnel raining down.

Engella returned fire, and managed to hit one guard in the chest, sending him crashing backwards. Injured, the guard broke away from the others, but he was able to tap a console on the wall as he fled. 'Get out!' he yelled, as he limped through the open door. The other guards were quick to follow – while the last guard out sealed the door behind him.

At first Engella didn't understand why they'd fallen back, but her confusion was quickly replaced by dread as a hatch opened in the centre of the ceiling.

She watched in horror as three shiny black spheres dropped down, hovering like a swarm of angry wasps ready to attack. Yet their sting would be far more terrible.

The first drone's red eye blinked as it scanned the

α β γ

corridor, looking for its target. A single camera lens focussed and whirred, while its main body began to hum, as it sent a signal to the others to follow its plan of attack.

The noise increased as their exoskeletons glowed blue, then white.

They became louder – and brighter too – as the explosives inside prepared to blow.

Engella shrieked and ran towards the opposite exit, scrambling at the door panel to try and escape. But the doors were sealed shut. She had no way out.

The drones triangulated Engella's position and suddenly zoomed at her.

The blast would certainly kill her.

Engella pounded on the door, and was shocked as it slid open to reveal a guard in full HuntCorp uniform standing there, his visor reflecting the glow of the floating bombs from above.

What now?

Engella covered her head, preparing for the worst, but the hum of the drones suddenly subsided. She turned back to see their lights blinking out, before each one dropped like lead to the floor, bouncing along the shiny tiles with a clatter.

'This way,' the guard said in a familiar accent,

gesturing for Engella to follow. He led her into a side corridor, where he proceeded to remove a small panel from one of the walls. 'Quick, get in,' he said.

Engella didn't need to be told twice and clambered in, quickly followed by the guard, who closed the panel behind them.

He placed his finger on his lip, telling her to remain quiet without saying a word. Engella did as she was told and listened as a troop of guards stamped by.

'We're safe in here,' the guard whispered, once the guards had passed. 'It's completely off the grid ... only place in the whole compound, too.'

Engella nodded and waited patiently for him to continue.

'Long time no see,' the guard said, as he removed his helmet.

Engella's mouth dropped wide open. 'Eddie?!' I can't believe it!'

He was no longer a boy but a young man. He was tall and toned, but he was still recognisable from his big brown eyes and curls of black hair. He was clean-shaven, although his dark stubble had already started to grow back.

'You're all grown up!' Engella said, laughing. 'How long has it been?'

'Five years, give or take a few months. Who's the kid now, kiddo?' Eddie said, showing off his shiny white teeth. 'Don't worry, I've got your back, you're safe here.'

His use of words reminded Engella of something, but it took her a few moments to remember exactly what it was. It suddenly all came flooding back. 'Wait a minute ...' she said. I know your voice ... You! You're the guy on the phone, who helped me!'

'What are you talking about?' Eddie asked, perplexed.

'Don't you remember?' said Engella. 'In New Shanghai?'

'Where?'

Engella knew instantly that Eddie had no idea what she was talking about, and she remembered her conversation with Patrick.

Eddie had no idea, because those events hadn't happened for him yet.

Engella considered this carefully. *The rules.*

She decided to change the subject. 'What happened to your town, and how did you end up here?'

'HuntCorp killed my mom,' Eddie said bluntly, his face full of sadness.

Engella gasped and placed her hand on his shoulder, but he pulled away. 'I'm so sorry, Eddie.'

'It's not your fault ... In fact, it's mine. I kept the

photos … and the Hunters came looking for them. I should have listened to Annys.'

Engella nodded unsure what to say next, when Eddie broke the silence. 'I'm okay though,' he said. 'Well, I'm getting there. It still hurts like hell, but I guess it always will.'

Engella leaned forwards. 'What happened to you then?' she asked.

'After they did that to Mom, I was a mess. I knew I wouldn't be able to stop until I found out who did it, and the only way to truly know what happened was to get on the inside. That's when I joined the guard.'

Engella considered what she had heard before she continued. 'Did you find out who did it?'

Eddie looked Engella directly in the eyes. 'I had everything planned out, Engella. I was about to get the name, then the alarms went off and this place went crazy. I checked the monitors and saw you were under attack. I obviously couldn't leave you.'

Engella was taken aback by this. 'Well I'm grateful that you did.'

'I was so close. I was going to download HuntCorp's entire memory core … intelligence … historical data … everything. But since you activated the security systems they traced the hack I'd started. It won't be long before they link me to it … let's just say I'm pretty much screwed.'

'Let me help you.'

'It's too late … my security access has already been restricted, which means they're onto me. I don't have any options left.'

'I'm so sorry for messing up your plans … but I think I know how you're going to get out of this.'

'You do?'

'Yes, but I'll need your help first. I came here looking for Annys. She was captured by the Hunters and they brought her here. Have you seen her?'

Eddie looked up. 'Actually, yes – I have,' he said, smiling. 'I saw she'd been arrested a few days ago, so I managed to get assigned to her cell block – through a little hack, of course. I've already given her a helping hand, but you'll need to get her outside.'

Engella had a moment of realisation. Her mind was blown. Everything had been linked. She reached inside her rucksack and pulled out the box of shiftbands.

'What's that?' asked Eddie.

'Your ticket out of here,' said Engella, grinning. 'But first thing's first … what's the quickest route to the prison barracks? And how would I find the memory core you mentioned?'

Eddie shook his head and pursed his lips. 'It's too late, Engella. The primary core will be overrun by now … I'd already hacked the security systems, but they'll have blocked all access by now. The only way would be … nah. It's impossible.'

'What?'

'Well … you'd have to do everything manually, meaning you'd need to plug this hack directly into a console.' He held out a small data chip engraved with the HuntCorp insignia. 'It's too dangerous Engella … that boat has sailed.'

'It's worth a try, right?'

Eddie paused, then smiled at Engella. 'Maybe it is …' he said reluctantly, before handing Engella the data chip. 'It's already loaded up with everything you need. You just have to plug it in.'

Engella nodded, and placed the data chip into her pocket. 'Thanks Eddie, I'll do my best. Now – about your ticket out of here …' She reached for the box of shiftbands and opened the lid.

'What are they?' Eddie asked, as he peered at the shiftbands inside.

'Take your pick,' Engella said.

Eddie hesitated, his hand hovering over the shiftbands before finally choosing Gamma.

'I have a feeling you're going to need this too,' Engella said, as she passed Eddie her journal. 'It's all in there – times, places, events. Everything that has happened to me. Well, thinking about it ... some of it *will* happen for you. You have quite a lot of work ahead of you.'

'I don't understand,' Eddie said.

'You will ... soon.'

'I'll try my best.'

'Don't worry, Eddie ... you did great. Erm, I mean, you're *going to* do great.'

Engella paused, and reached inside her rucksack. 'Hold on,' she said. 'Can you do one more thing for me?' She handed Eddie the replicator pack she'd purchased from CLONEPETZ. 'Read my journal, everything you'll need is in there.'

Eddie nodded and looked down at the shiftband in his hand. 'How do I use this thing?' he asked.

He reached out his arm and allowed Engella to place the shiftband around his wrist. She waved her hand over the device, and after showing Eddie how to enter space-time coordinates, she pointed out the relevant notes in her journal.

'If my memory serves me right, I'd say you're off to New Shanghai first. My past-self needs your help. She's counting on you.'

'Woah. This is pretty epic ... I'll try my best.'

She waved her hand over his shiftband. 'Ready to try another time tunnel?' she asked, grinning. 'Shift.'

A portal opened and they shielded their eyes from the glare. Eddie looked at the lights with anticipation, before turning to Engella. He smiled, and stepped through.

After the lights had faded away, Engella cleared her mind.

Focus.

She thought back to her first visit to Truth or Consequences, when Annys had used her V-Dis to make scans of the compound. Annys had told Engella that the data she'd recorded would be important one day.

It all made sense now. That day had arrived.

'There's no place like home,' Engella whispered into the device.

The shiftband chimed and a holographic projection appeared above. She waved her hands through the lights, zooming in and out until she found her current location within the holographic map of the compound.

She had everything she needed.

After discovering she was on the edge of a long service tunnel which snaked beneath the compound, she checked the walls to find a way inside. The map

α β γ

had the exit routes highlighted, all flashing in red. She was quick to locate the prison barracks on the map and plotted the shortest route to get there.

She now knew the way, she just had to make the trip.

She broke through another panel and climbed into the service tunnel.

It was dark and damp inside. Condensation dripped from the scorching pipes which lined the ceiling, while steam filled the passageway ahead.

Engella checked the route ahead, and noticed from her map that she'd pass relatively close to one of the compound's secondary computer cores. It wasn't the primary core that Eddie had mentioned, but it was a potential access point – so she decided to check it out. She sprinted into the shadows and made her way there.

After reaching the computer cores, she broke through the access panels and made her way inside. The room was deserted except for a tiny vacuum-bot which trundled around the room, picking up dirt and dust.

She raised her blaster and stayed close against the wall – in case any guards were hidden out of view.

She moved into the room and was surprised to find a man standing there in a white lab coat, holding a cup of coffee and a bright-pink iced donut. His round spectacles were nestled on the end of his nose and he stood completely still, too scared to move.

'Don't kill me!' the man said, as Engella pointed the blaster at him.

'I need to get past you,' Engella said. 'And I don't want to hurt anybody.'

The man nodded, and didn't dare say another word. Engella looked around to see a small laboratory on one side and an enclosed office on the other.

'How do I access the memory core from here?'

The man used his donut to gesture towards a console which protruded from the wall. 'You can access it from there,' he said with a stutter.

'Now get inside,' Engella said, as she gestured towards the office.

The man nodded and almost sprinted inside, spilling hot coffee over himself as he ran. Engella secured the door behind him, locking him inside, and ran to the console. She removed the data chip and plugged it directly into the computer.

The screen flashed with the HuntCorp insignia, but was quickly replaced with a range of strange symbols. Suddenly an animated skull with red flashing eyes and a wide grin flashed up, while a speech bubble appeared above: *You've been hacked by Cypher-16, have a nice day.*

Engella watched with glee as a series of files opened across the screen.

She pulled up the search function and typed in the first name that came to mind.

MAY NAKAMURA

She paused, almost too frightened to carry on, but she took a deep breath and commenced the search.

Data began to roll across the screen when a message flashed up in red lettering.

DELETION INCOMPLETE. PARADOX IDENTIFIED

Engella couldn't believe what she'd read. If deletion hadn't yet been completed, there was still a chance of finding her parents alive. A rush of motivation filled her, the knowledge she'd received pushing her forwards.

She checked the status of the download when a crash at the door startled her. She turned to see the man in round spectacles pulling a weapon from beneath the laboratory bench.

She barely had time to react and pulled out the data chip, rushing out from where she'd entered.

The urgency of Annys's rescue suddenly hit home. She made her way through the maze of service shafts, following the map which Annys had prepared for this day.

She blasted her way through the wall and fell through into the cell block to find Annys emerging.

'Now that's what I call an entrance!' Annys said, her eyes wide with joy. 'I knew you'd find me.'

'It looks like you know a lot of things,' Engella said, with a grin. 'I returned to Skye ... Patrick told me everything ... I've finally found my sister.'

Annys hugged Engella tightly and kissed her on the cheek. 'I'm sorry I couldn't tell you sooner.'

'It's okay, Annys, I understand.'

Annys's neck was purple and red, the bruise almost reaching her chin. 'What have they done to you?' Engella asked, furiously.

'It's nothing, dear ... I'll be okay.'

'We'd better get out of here,' Engella said, as she led Annys towards the exit. 'Cover your eyes ...'

She shot the door wide open, sending a thousand tiny metal pieces blasting outwards.

Engella grabbed Annys's hand and pulled her outside. They ran into the open courtyard, their vision blurred by the glare of the sun.

They prepared to shift, but Engella was disorientated by the rev of an engine. She turned to see a vehicle hurtling towards them. She reached over Annys, covering her from whoever was approaching, but was suddenly elated when she realised who it was.

'Get in!' Eddie yelled, as he flung open the side door. He was no longer wearing his HuntCorp uniform, but a T-shirt and jeans, a cap worn backwards and a scarf around his neck. His stubble had been replaced by a full beard.

'New Shanghai was awesome!' he said, grinning widely.

Annys piled in and reached out for Engella's hand, but she was too late.

Engella's head was wrenched backwards, her neck in the grip of a vicious Hunter.

'Go!' Engella shouted out, as she was wrestled to the ground.

ₒ   ₒ   ₒ

Eddie realised there was no time to help Engella, so he pushed his foot down on the accelerator and drove the vehicle towards the compound wall, the wheels sending a cloud of dust into the air.

Annys closed her eyes. 'I hope you know what you're doing dear!' she yelled.

Eddie smiled and said simply, 'Shift.'

The vehicle shuddered as it was pulled into a spinning vortex, only seconds before it would have crashed into the wall.

⚘   ⚘   ⚘

'You left me for dead,' Tala snapped, as she held Engella in a headlock. 'That was a big mistake.'

'I won't make the same mistake twice,' Engella yelled, squirming as she tried to find a way to escape.

Tala pressed her weight onto Engella's body, and rolled her onto her back, pushing her face into the sand until she gasped for breath.

'I never got to introduce myself the last time we met,' snarled the Hunter. 'You'll be sorry you ever crossed me.'

Lera Tox ran into the courtyard to find Tala crushing Engella.

'I'll take her into custody now, Commander,' Lera said.

'Not this time,' Tala replied. 'This one's mine.' She removed a knife from her belt and placed both knees onto Engella's chest.

'Commander,' Lera said. 'We can take the prisoner into custody now...' But her words fell on deaf ears.

Tala pushed the knife against Engella's throat.

'Commander!' Lera yelled, as she pulled Tala's arm away. 'I said we're ready to secure the prisoner!'

With Tala distracted, Engella was able to break free of her hold, and waved her hand across her wrist, adding in a random timepoint in the process.

She yelled out with everything she could muster ... 'Shift!'

A vortex rushed around them like a spinning tornado, throwing sand and stones into the air, and Engella, Lera, and Tala were all dragged inside.

β ϙ
PORTAL

The spherical portal of the wormhole's interior twisted and turned through space-time, flashing on all sides, as times gone by and times yet to be flowed past them like leaves on a river. They tumbled in a spiral; spinning, turning, unable to control which way they fell. Tala held Engella in a tight embrace, her arms wrapped around her waist, but Engella kicked away, sending Tala spinning towards the edge of the vortex.

Lera tumbled behind them and placed her arms by her sides like a skydiver, managing to creep closer to the duelling foes ahead. She reached out and grabbed Tala's arm, pulling her away from Engella. Tala turned her vile stare towards her junior and kicked out with everything she had, pushing Lera to the portal's edge. Lera's eyes were wide with shock: the commander had lost all sense now – her revenge on Engella now coming above all else, even if it meant attacking one of her own.

Lera screamed out as gravity dragged her out of the wormhole. She would be killed instantly – vaporised in space-time – so she only had one option. She allowed herself to fall away, and tumbled out of space-time, falling into an unknown time and place.

Engella looked into Lera's terrified eyes as she fell out of the slipstream, not knowing if she'd survive the fall.

Tala returned her foul gaze to Engella, who she grabbed at again, but Engella managed to kick her away. Howling in pain, Tala pulled back.

Sensing the opportunity, Engella deactivated her shiftband, and they materialised out of space-time a few feet in the air, ploughing down to the ground with a thump.

They had now fallen several decades into the past, and had arrived at a time before the original compound had been constructed. They tried to keep their balance but the winds were too strong. They'd found themselves on a plateau beside a rocky precipice, towards the highest peak of Turtleback Mountain. Stones, rocks and dust littered the ground.

Tala held her knife firmly and dived towards Engella, who managed to roll out of the way.

'It doesn't have to end this way,' Engella said, as she prepared herself for the onslaught.

'You know it does,' Tala snapped, her face like thunder. 'You killed my family, and now I'll kill you.'

Engella stepped backwards, stunned. 'I don't know what you're talking about!' she yelled over the howling wind.

'You killed them in cold blood ... murderer!' Tala bounded forwards, and jabbed the knife towards Engella managing to scrape her arm.

Engella pulled away in pain and could feel the wetness of the blood as it dripped inside her sleeve.

'I didn't kill anybody,' Engella yelled. 'You've got it all wrong!'

Tala screamed out in rage and charged at Engella, crashing into her headfirst. They fought, and this time Engella finally had the upper hand, pushing Tala away and sending her crashing to the ground.

'You're a liar!' Tala snarled, as she struggled away. 'You attacked New Shanghai with a fleet of drones. My family didn't stand a chance!'

They got to their feet, and Tala charged again, but this time Engella was prepared, and used Tala's own force against her – sending them both smashing towards the cliff's edge.

But they'd miscalculated, and the force knocked them both over the side.

All they could do was scream out, as they plunged into the void below.

Engella, as she twisted through the air, had only one choice. She activated her shiftband and light flickered from her wrist.

'Help me!' Tala yelled, as she realised her own shiftband wasn't working.

Engella didn't have time to react before the vortex engulfed her. She tried to reach out, but Tala was already too far away.

As the lights glared brightly, Engella looked into Tala's eyes one last time. Eyes once so full of hatred now looked back with an expression of pure fear and desperation, as she fell into the precipice below.

β ⚲

1998-JAN-22 15:25

RUBHA SHLÈITE, SKYE, SCOTLAND

Engella held her head, expecting to hit the rocks below, but she'd managed to shift in time, and had appeared in a very familiar place. She checked her coordinates and realised that over forty years had passed since her last visit.

At first she was confused, and then everything began to make sense. She'd shifted without setting coordinates again, and as she had already discovered, the shiftbands had been programmed to arrive at these coordinates if that had happened.

She thought of Tala and felt a wave of guilt. She was in a state of shock, as she'd never wanted to hurt anyone. But she'd had no choice.

She watched as waves crashed against the beach. The memories of her family returned; building sandcastles and eating ice cream. But this time, she remembered Annys's face.

The day when they'd met on this very beach.

She was about to follow the route to the cottage when a familiar figure came into view. She ran forwards to get a closer look, and her eyes beamed when she realised who it was.

The woman was walking a chocolate Labrador who was jumping across the sand.

'Annys?' Engella yelled, as she ran towards her sister.

'Engella, my dear, it's been a very long time! Well, it must be over forty years, by now ... I've been waiting for you.'

The chocolate Labrador ran up to Engella, his tail wagging.

'Oh, Rupert!' Engella said, as she hugged him. 'I've missed you so much.'

Engella patted Rupert on the head and turned to Annys. 'I'm so sorry,' she said. 'I promised Patrick I'd come back. But I'm too late.'

'My dear, you have nothing to be sorry about. You've arrived exactly when you were supposed to arrive. None of us have any control over what happens. Patrick taught me that. In fact, he told me everything he knew about space-time travel. It was always supposed to happen like this.'

'And Patrick knew that, didn't he?' Engella asked, but she already knew the answer. 'When we said our goodbyes, he knew I wouldn't see him again.'

Annys reached into her coat pocket and pulled out the inhibitor. 'Patrick left me a note, before he passed. He told me to switch this off on this date – today that is – and when I did, you'd appear. He said you'd need my help.'

'Patrick was a good man.'

'Indeed, he was. He was like a father to me. He had a good life here, don't you worry.'

Engella nodded.

'Now dear, I bet you have a lot to tell me.'

They talked about the events which had led Engella back to the beach that day. She shared stories of things to come, events which were in this Annys's future. Events that one day, when they were supposed to, would eventually come to pass.

'It makes my head hurt,' said Annys.

'Tell me about it,' said Engella. 'But remember. Don't say a thing to my past-self when she arrives. She'll know everything when she's supposed to know it.'

'The rules?' asked Annys.

'Yes, Annys, the rules. If you tell my past-self about any of this, things may not happen as they're supposed to.'

'I'll remember,' said Annys. 'You're so strong, dear. I couldn't do any of this without you.'

Engella placed her hand on Annys's shoulder and hugged her tightly. 'And I couldn't have done any of this without you ... If I remember correctly, my past-self will be arriving on the beach very soon. Shall we?'

'Yes, dear.'

Engella led her sister to the right point on the beach, where the waves crashed and the seagulls hovered on the upwind, and played with Rupert as they walked.

Soon, Engella knew it was the right time to leave.

'You'll be right here, waiting for me.'

'I'll be here. You, my dear, need to move on with your life now. You have a lot to do. Goodbye.'

Engella moved up the hillside so she could have a better view of the events below. She watched as Annys wandered along the sea's edge, while Rupert splashed through the surf.

A flash of light caught her attention, and she

watched with amazement as a vortex flashed in the centre of the beach, while her past-self fell through the portal, and lay unconscious in the sand.

Although it was strange to say it, she rather envied her past-self, who was about to begin an adventure like no other.

The events of the last few days, months and years would all happen like they were supposed to. The connections had been made, linked through space-time. Still, she couldn't quite get her head around it.

Engella left the beach, and found somewhere quiet to shift away. She'd forgotten one important thing. She was supposed to ask Patrick to calibrate the shiftbands, but it had slipped her mind. In her haste to leave, she carelessly set a random timepoint.

The shiftband, unable to target the correct coordinates, began to decelerate rapidly – time falling backwards at an unprecedented speed, and Engella, completely unaware any of it was happening, tumbled into the past.

βγδ♂
Pleistocene era (43,785 Before Present)

Engella shifted out into the open air, a few metres above the ground. She fell downwards, and put her hands out to break her fall, but she smashed into the snow and ice with a thud, knocking her head in the process. She groaned in pain and could barely move, too dizzy to get up, so she just lay there and thought about her family.

Her parents and her sister too.

Will I ever see them again?

She opened her eyes, but her vision was blurred so she closed them again. She was disorientated, with a mild concussion, and it wasn't long before she passed out.

She awoke. She wasn't sure how long she'd been out for, but the snow had been falling heavily during this time, as her legs were now partially covered. She shivered – her body was losing heat at a dangerous rate, her breathing shallower by the minute.

She passed out again, but quickly came around as a figure stumbled towards her through the snow.

Engella tried to see who it was, but she couldn't make out their face.

Closing her eyes, she fought against the deep slumber which tried to engulf her.

She opened her eyes again, and this time saw a face up close; a person watching over her.

'Engella. You need to get up. It's very important,' the woman said. 'You need to get up, now.'

Engella reached out and touched the face to feel the warmth of her skin. 'Mama?' she asked. 'I thought you were gone.'

'I'm here darling. I'll always be with you. Now, you must get up. You have so many important things to do. I'm waiting for you.'

Engella opened her eyes and reached out for her mother, but there was no one there.

Her head throbbed but she felt better, and warm, considering the place she had ended up.

α β γ δ

She reviewed the data on her shiftband and realised she'd travelled far into the ancient past, and by the looks of the snow and ice around her, it was the middle of the Ice Age. She sat up, too quickly at first as pain returned to her temples – so she slowed down, and lay on her side.

The sun began to rise in the east, giving the barren landscape of snow and ice a warm glow.

They'll find me. I know they will.

Annys was her family now, and she had to fight the cold to make sure she'd see her again. For the first time in years, she had family. She had found her sister and that was enough to keep her going.

She covered her eyes to block out the glare of the sun.

But then, something in the distance caught her attention. A glint, far away, like the reflection of light off metal. It was gone before she could identify where it was coming from.

But there it was again. Another flash and much closer this time, reflecting the sun.

The lights of a wormhole glowed on the ice beside her, melting the snow into a puddle, and two figures emerged.

Annys and Eddie had found her.

'Engella!' Annys yelled as she ran to her sister,

covering her in a checked sheet, while Eddie brought over a bottle of water, and passed her some to drink.

'I thought we'd lost you, dear,' said Annys as she held her close, kissing her on the cheek.

Their eyes welled up, and they began to cry.

They wept – finally reunited after so many years. They'd found each other, at last. Separated by years. Through time and through space.

Eddie removed his scarf, and wrapped it around Engella's neck.

'How did you find me?' Engella asked.

'The smartphone,' Eddie said. 'I placed a transmitter inside, just in case.'

Engella reached inside her top pocket and pulled it out. 'This has turned out to be my lucky charm!'

Eddie helped Engella to her feet and, once she was strong enough to walk, they prepared to make their move.

Annys raised her eyebrows. 'I think it's time we got out of here,' she said. 'My ancient palaeontology isn't up to scratch, but I'm sure there are a few beasties from this era that we'd want to avoid.'

Engella looked pensive. 'The Hunters,' she said. 'They won't stop coming for us until they have our shiftbands.'

'We have a lot of work to do before I'm ready to give up mine,' said Eddie. 'I need to find out who killed my mom.'

Engella nodded. 'And I won't stop until I've found my parents.' She turned to Annys. 'Sorry. Once we've found *our* parents.'

'Hear hear,' said Annys, smiling.

Engella reached inside her pocket. 'I suggest we start with this...' she said, holding out the data chip. 'I managed to download the Hunters' memory core. Well, most of it, anyway.'

Eddie rushed forwards, his eyes wide. 'Engella! That's incredible.'

'Sorry I messed up your plans,' Engella said.

'It doesn't matter anymore,' said Eddie. 'We have everything we need now, thanks to you.'

Engella turned to Annys. 'Our parents are out there somewhere,' she said. 'I just know it. We can't leave them ... they're counting on us. How about we go on one more adventure, before we find somewhere safe to settle down?'

'Sounds good to me, dear.'

'Eddie?'

'Sounds like a plan to me.'

Annys put her arms on Engella's shoulders. 'As

long as you promise me one thing, dear... we stick together this time, okay?'

Engella took Annys's hand. 'Deal.'

'Oh, I almost forgot. We have someone very special for you to meet,' said Eddie, as he reached for his backpack. 'I went to the cottage and he was right where you'd said he would be. Poor boy. But I took a cutting of his hair, and after a bit of magic with that replication pack you gave me...'

Engella's eyes lit up, and she watched as the backpack shuffled from side to side.

Eddie placed it on the floor, opening the lid, and Engella could see a face peeping out from the top.

The chocolate Labrador puppy bounded out of the backpack, and skipped towards Engella, his tail wagging and his tongue hanging out.

'Rupert!' yelled Engella. 'You made him!'

'Introducing Rupert II,' said Eddie.

Annys patted the puppy on the head, while Engella hugged him tightly.

'Thank you, dear,' said Annys. 'He's as playful as his older brother always was. It's all in the genes, I guess. But I do need to ask you one thing ... why on earth does he glow in the dark?'

Engella laughed. 'Oh! Yeah ... about that.'

Annys chuckled, and reached out. 'I think it's time to go,' she said.

'I don't know where we'll end up next,' said Engella. 'But I'm looking forward to the trip.'

They huddled together and held hands, their faces bright with joy, their laughs echoing throughout the icy tundra.

'Let's do this,' said Eddie.

'Shift,' said Engella.

Their portal opened, glowing and glistening like a diamond on the hillside.

Engella had no idea what was coming next, but she was sure about one thing.

She'd never leave her sister's side again.

β Q

1955-SEP-16 11:19
RUBHA SHLÈITE, SKYE, SCOTLAND

They were seated in the sitting room, in front of the fireplace which burned brightly, when Annika turned to Patrick. 'Patrick?' she asked, as she gazed at a photo of them stood outside the cottage. 'I like this photo of you and I, but I wish we had a photo of Engella too.'

'What did we say about my name, Annika?'

'Sorry, I forgot. Grandpa.'

'That's okay. I'm sure it'll get easier with time. But we must remember why it's important. Engella needs us to keep this place a secret. Do you remember why?'

'So the bad people won't be able to find us?'

'That's right.' Patrick hadn't wanted to tell Annika about the Hunters at such a young age. Yet, he knew he wouldn't be around for ever, so it was important that she understood the importance of their secret.

Annika sat with her legs hanging over the sofa, and swung them wildly. 'Pat ... Oops. I mean, Grandpa?'

'Yes, darling?'

'Will we ever see Engella again?'

'Yes, you definitely will. In fact, one day, you'll need to do something very important. Engella will need your help. So, I need you to promise you'll be very brave. I want you to watch over her for me. Will you do that?'

'Yes Grandpa, I promise.'

Patrick smiled. 'I knew I could count on you.'

'I'll be her watcher,' Annika said.

Patrick put his arms around her, and hugged her tightly. 'Good girl. Now, let's try it again, shall we? Hello. Pleased to meet you. What's your name?'

'Hello, nice to meet you too. My name's Annys Munro.'

'Hello, Annys. And where do you live?'

'I live in Elgol Cottage, with my grandpa.'

'Well done, dear. We'll get used to saying it eventually, it'll just take a little time.'

'Will this mean the bad people won't be able to find us?'

'You don't need to worry about them, I can promise you that,' Patrick said. He reached into his pocket and pulled something out. It glistened as it reflected the flames from the fireplace.

'Annys, I have something for you. It's a present – from Engella. It's a very special bracelet. She wants you to have it so you'll always remember how special you are to her.'

'Is it a daisy chain?!' Annys asked, her eyes wide with excitement.

'Oh, it's even more special than a daisy chain,' Patrick said, as he placed the glistening shiftband on her wrist. 'Happy birthday, dear.'

'Thank you, Grandpa, oh – and Engella too! I love it.'

'So, I've been waiting to tell you something. Remember, last year, when Engella visited us? Do you remember those special lights?'

'Yes, they were so pretty. Engella made them, didn't she?'

'That's right. What I'm about to tell you, well, it's quite remarkable really. Let's sit down and get comfortable. How about I pour us a cup of Earl Grey, and I can tell you all about it.'

The little girl was startled by a clatter from the alleyway, and a bright flash that twinkled away. The lights were pretty, like stars as they glistened in the night sky. At first, she had been frightened in case the bad people had returned. She'd been told by her papa to avoid strangers at all costs, so she hid in the shadows behind a refuse container. She sat with her back against the cold metal and faced the wall and stayed as quiet as a mouse.

The walls were plastered with old posters. She looked up to see that one of them had a photo of a cute dog, who reminded her of Toto, a character from her favourite holomovie.

She smiled as she remembered her papa when he used to read stories to her. Once she was sure that the coast was clear, she peered out from behind the bin.

Flickers of light illuminated the brick walls of the buildings. The little girl was intrigued, but she couldn't see where the lights were coming from, so she edged a little closer. She stepped out from behind the container, and discovered a small silver cube on the ground.

She edged closer, still unsure whether or not to approach. She picked it up, uncertain of what she'd found.

Light was shining from the cube's top panel.

A *holocube*, she thought.

She watched with joy as the hologram began to play, her eyes wide with excitement. She let out a giggle, as she realised it was her favourite holomovie, and watched with joy as Dorothy skipped along the yellow-brick road.

The Wizard of Oz. It had always been her favourite.

She rushed forwards, and lay herself flat on the ground, her face in her hands, her eyes wide, and her grin reaching from cheek to cheek.

The hologram played through, before it flickered and started again.

She picked up the device, as she was determined to keep it as her own, and gasped as she noticed something etched into the bottom.

Keep looking. We'll find you. ER.

The little girl began to sob; she just couldn't hold back the tears. She cried aloud, and tears flooded down her face.

Papa. I knew you'd find me.

There were also several symbols etched beneath, but she didn't know what they meant. She knew it was probably important. A message from her parents, or a clue to help her find them.

The little girl held the holocube tightly. This was the closest she'd felt to her parents for over a year. She knew this place was important, which was why she'd stayed there. But, she didn't yet know why.

She'd been looking for something – anything – that might help her find her parents, and finally she'd found something. The message was what she'd been looking for. She'd lost her parents, but they'd lost her too.

The message gave her hope. The hope to keep looking, however hard it would be, and whatever the cost. She felt stronger that day.

She deactivated the holocube and placed it in her pocket. She skipped out of the alleyway into the sunlight, her expression bright and joyful.

After reaching a lawn surrounded by flowers, she sat down and removed her journal from her rucksack. She sketched some notes, being sure to record the place and time, listing every detail she could remember.

Soon, the little girl decided it was time to move again. She couldn't stay in one place for too long, or the bad people would find her. Her parents had taught her this was very important. She waved her hand over the metal band around her wrist, and she was enveloped in a flash of light.

She looked back, one last time. She'd return to this place – she just knew it – but for now, she was at peace.

That day, she felt a little closer to her parents. She finally had hope of finding them again.

And one day, however far away, the little girl knew they'd find each other again.

It was only a matter of time.

ACKNOWLEDGEMENTS

I discovered early on in my publishing journey that every book is a team effort, so bear with me while I remember everyone who has helped me to make this the best book it could possibly be.

First of all thanks to my family: my mum, Sandra, my nan, Vicky and my sister Michelle, as well as my brother-in-law Chris and my nephew Hayden.

This story is the last in a long line of drafts, and originated from a short story I published in 2016, called *Engella*. Thank you to Alison Rasmussen, who illustrated the original short story, and to everyone who read it; helping the story to make the charts in the process, and even getting me into my local newspaper.

Those early reviews and the support from my readers helped me to develop enough confidence to attempt the challenge of writing a novel. Special thanks to Corine Barnes, Tammy Davey, Gabriella Farmer, Jon Laight, Donna Levett, Tina and Amanda Morley, Shawnta Neal, Debra Schwitzer and Mandy Walkden-Brown.

To Roisin Heycock, my developmental editor, who helped me develop the manuscript through several versions, and thanks to my copy-editors Emma Mitchell and Rachel Mann for helping me to perfect the text.

To all of my friends who acted as beta readers, helping me to develop the final draft: James Dobbyn, Dominika Kronsteiner, Jessica Metzelaar-McGee, Catherine Mullan, Amy Schou and Tracey Van Wyk. And a special shout out to my talented author friends who also acted as beta readers: Lesley Hayes and Sylva Fae.

To Patrick Knowles, who designed the most wonderfully eye-catching cover, and to Maya Tatsukawa who did the most beautiful interior book design (I wonder if anyone has spotted the secret code inside – a hint to the future, perhaps?).

Thank you to Rachel Gilbey for arranging my blog

tour and to all the writers, reviewers and bloggers who have already been so supportive. And a special thanks also goes to Tamara and Clare at Moon Lane Books, for letting me have my book launch in your wonderful shop.

Thank you, readers, for choosing to read my book.

And last but by no means least thank you to Adrian, my best friend and partner, for taking me on so many adventures around the world and to so many amazing places – many of which have made it into this story, such as our first holiday together to the Isle of Skye. Your support got me through so many challenges and I'm forever grateful.

And thanks to Engella, Annys and Eddie for finally going quiet in my head – their thoughts and words finally down on the pages of this book.

But I can hear them stirring again already, so I doubt it'll be long before their adventures begin again...

It'll only be a matter of time, I'm sure.

PAUL IAN CROSS is an award-winning children's author and scientist from London, UK.

Paul works in clinical research (developing new medicines) and he's also involved in science communication – presenting science to non-scientists. He enjoys his science career but he has a real passion for writing stories! He enjoys introducing children to the wonders of science, especially reluctant readers. By introducing science creatively, he aims to spark their interest, allowing them to gain confidence with their reading. As a previous reluctant reader himself, he understands how hard it can be. But it's all about making reading fun and interesting!

In his spare time, Paul loves visiting new and exciting places where he's always looking for his next story. One of his favourite places is Scotland, especially the Isle of Skye. His latest adventures include a trip to Japan as well as two months travelling around the South Pacific – including Los Angeles, French Polynesia, New Zealand, Australia and the Cook Islands.

Connect with Paul Ian Cross
www.pauliancross.com
Twitter: @tyrannopaulus
Facebook: /pauliancrossauthor
Instagram: @pauliancross.author